LAST ONE IN IS . . .

McCullough entered first, then Hollis. They turned to assist Berryman then and had a hand under each armpit when it happened.

His radio went into a howl of oscillation as four voices tried to use it at the same time, and McCullough saw aliens swarming toward them out of the dark spaces between the supposedly solid masses of equipment. The colonel had lost his spotlight, and Berryman was being pulled away from them.

One of the aliens had anchored itself to the combing with two of its tentacles while the other two were wrapped around the pilot's feet. Another e-t had swarmed onto his back, its sting jabbing furiously—McCullough could hear it clanking against Berryman's air tanks. *He knew that it had only to shift its position by a few inches for the pilot to be very horribly dead. And there was nothing he could do to stop it . . .*

All
Judgment
Fled

JAMES WHITE

A Del Rey Book

BALLANTINE BOOKS • NEW YORK

A Del Rey Book
Published by Ballantine Books

Library of Congress Catalog Card Number: 70-86388

ISBN 0-345-28025-3

Manufactured in the United States of America

First Edition: September 1970
Second Printing: April 1979

First Canadian Printing: October 1970

Cover art by Wayne Douglas Barlowe

ALL JUDGMENT FLED

chapter one

∿∾ ୨୧ ∿∾ ୨୧ ∿∾

O judgment, thou art fled to brutish beasts,
And men have lost their reason.

Shakespeare

IT ALL BEGAN with a small scratch on a time exposure
of some star clouds in Saggitarius and its presence
was blamed on mishandling or faulty processing. But
a second exposure of the same area showed a similar
scratch which began where the first one had left off
and traced a path which was unmistakably curved,
indicating that it was altering its own trajectory and
could not therefore be a natural celestial body. Immediately every instrument which could be brought
to bear was directed at the Ship.

The largest optical instruments showed only a
point of light, spectro-analysis indicated a highly re-
flective surface suggestive of metal and the great
bowls of the radio telescopes gathered nothing at all.
By this time the Ship had taken up an orbit some
twelve million miles beyond the orbit of Mars, still

1

without making any attempt to communicate, and the decision was taken to sacrifice the Jupiter probe in an attempt to gain more information about the intruder.

The complex and horribly expensive piece of hardware which was the Jupiter Probe—the unmanned observatory for the examination of the Jovian system which was to have relayed its data to Earth for decades to come—was at that time relatively close to the alien ship. It was thought that if the fuel reserve to be used for maneuvering inside the Jovian system was used for an immediate and major course correction, the probe could be made to pass within fifty thousand miles of the stranger.

As a result, there was relayed back to Earth a low definition picture of the vessel which orbited silently and, some thought, implacably, like some tremendous battleship cruising off the coast of a tiny, backward island. It made no signal nor did it reply in any recognizable fashion to those which were being made. For the probe's instruments showed the object to be metallic, shaped like a blunt torpedo with a pattern of bulges encircling its midsection, and just under half a mile long.

Inevitably there were those who wanted an even closer look, and two small, sophisticated dugout canoes were hastily modified and readied for launching.

"It seems to me," said Walters very seriously, "that we have not gone far enough into the philosophical implications of this thing. At present that ship is a Mystery, but once we make contact it will then become a Problem. There's a difference, you know."

"Not really," Berryman said in a matching tone.

"A problem is simply a mystery which has been broken down into a number of handy pieces, some of which are usually related to problems already solved. And far be it from me to impugn the thought processes of a fellow officer, but your stand smacks of intellectual cowardice."

"Advocating a greater degree of caution and prior mental preparation is not cowardice," Walters returned, "and if we're to begin impugning minds, it's my opinion that too much confidence—you can call it bravery if you like—is in itself a form of instability which . . ."

"What sort of twisted mind is it that can insult a man by calling him brave?" said Berryman, laughing. "It seems to me everyone on this operation wants to be the psychologist except the psychologist. What do you say, Doctor?"

McCullough was silent for a moment. He was wondering what insensitive idiot it had been who had first likened the horrible sensation he was feeling in his stomach to butterflies. But he knew that the other two men were verbally whistling in the dark and in the circumstances he could do nothing less than make it a trio. He said, "I'm not a psychologist and anyway my couch is full at the moment—I'm in it . . ."

"Sorry to interrupt, gentlemen," said Control suddenly. *"I have to tell you that Colonel Morrison's ship had a three-minute hold at minus eighteen minutes, so your takeoff will not now be simultaneous. Is this understood? Your own countdown is proceeding and is at minus sixty seconds . . . now!"*

"Command pilot here," said Berryman. "Understood. Tell the colonel last man to touch the alien ship is a . . ."

"Don't you think you are all working a little too hard at projecting the image of fearless, dedicated scientists exchanging airy persiflage within seconds of being hurled into the unknown? Your upper lips must be so stiff I'm surprised you can still talk with them. Would you agree that you may be overcompensating for a temporary and quite understandable anxiety neurosis?

"Minus twenty seconds and counting . . . eighteen, seventeen, sixteen . . ."

"You're right, Walters," said Berryman. "*Everybody* wants to be a psychologist!"

"Twelve, eleven, ten . . ."

"I want off," said Walters.

"At minus seven seconds are you kidding! Four, three, two, one . . ."

The acceleration built up until McCullough was sure his body could take no more, and still it increased. Even his eyes felt egg-shaped and his stomach seemed to be rammed tightly against his backbone. How anything as fragile as a butterfly could survive such treatment surprised him, but they were still fluttering away like mad—until accelerating ceased and his vision cleared, that is, and he was able to look outside. Only then did they become still, paralyzed like himself with wonder.

Control and guidance during this most critical stage of the trip was the responsibility of brains both human and electronic on the ground. Their short period of weightlessness ended as the second stage ignited, its three G's feeling almost comfortable after the beating he had taken on the way up. With his head still turned toward the port McCullough watched the splendor of the sunset line slide past below them to be replaced by the great, woolly darkness that was the cloud-covered Pacific.

Against this velvet blackness a tiny shooting star fell away from rather than toward Earth—Morrison's ship. He knew it was the colonel's ship because its flare died precisely three minutes after their own second stage cut out.

If everything had gone as planned—a very big if, despite the advances made since Apollo—they were now on a collision course with the sixty-million-miles-distant Ship. A period of decelleration, already precalculated, would ensure that the collision would be a gentle one, if they managed to collide with it at all. For the alien vessel was a perfect example of a point in space. It had position but no magnitude, no detectable radiation, no gravitational field to help suck them in if their course happened to be just a little off.

The thought of missing the alien vessel completely or having to use so much fuel finding it that they might not be able to return home, was to worry McCullough occasionally. Usually he tried, as he was doing now, to think about something else.

He could no longer see Morrison's ship. Either it was too small to be picked out by the naked eye—at least by McCullough's middle-aged, slightly astigmatic naked eye—or it was hidden by the glare from the monsoon season cloud blanket covering Africa and the South Atlantic. But suddenly the colonel was very much with them.

"*P-One calling P-Two. Come in, P-Two. How do you read?*"

"P-Two here," said Berryman, and laughed. "Almost deafening, sir, and as clear as the notes of a silver trumpet blowing the Last P—I mean Reveille . . ."

"Freudian slip," murmured Walters.

"*Loud and clear is good enough, Berryman— purple passages waste oxygen. Have you completed checking your pressurization and life-support systems?*"

"Yes, sir. All are Go."

"*Good. Take off your suits and all of you get some sleep as soon as possible. Use medication if necessary. At the present time I consider it psychologically desirable for a number of reasons, so go to sleep before your nasty little subconsciouses realize they've left home. That's an order, gentlemen. Good night.*"

A few minutes later, while the other two were helping him out of his suit, Walters said drily, "Even the colonel wants to be one," and Berryman added, "The trouble, Doctor, is that your psychologist's club is not sufficiently exclusive"

But the command pilot was wrong in one respect at least. McCullough now belonged to the most exclusive club on Earth, membership of which was reserved for that very select group of individuals who at some time had left the aforementioned planet. And like all good clubs or monastic orders or crack regiments, there were certain rules of behavior to follow. For even in the present day, members could find themselves in serious trouble, very serious trouble.

When this happened they were supposed to follow precedents established by certain founder members who had been similarly unfortunate. They were expected to talk quietly and keep control of themselves until all hope was gone, then perhaps smash their radios so that their wives and friends would not be distressed by their shouting for the help which nobody could possibly give them when their air gave out or their vehicle began to melt around them on re-entry.

During the five and a half months it would take them to reach the Ship, they would eat, sleep, talk and sweat within a few inches of each other. McCullough wondered if their club's rules of behavior, or esprit de corps or whatever peculiar quality it was that made a group of individuals greater than the sum of its parts, would keep them from suiciding out of sheer loneliness or tearing each other to pieces from utter boredom or disintegrating into madness and death for reasons they could not as yet even imagine.

McCullough hoped it would. He was almost sure it would.

chapter two

THE PROMETHEUS PROJECT was either the result of some very devious thinking or there had been introduced into it such a multiplicity of objectives that its planners did not know where they were. Even allowing for the hasty mounting of the operation—the original purpose of the two ships was to have been the setting up of a manned lab and observatory on Deimos—McCullough's instructions were a mishmash of insufficient data and ambiguous language.

He could follow their reasoning and even feel sympathy for their problem. The alien vessel beyond the orbit of Mars was an enigma. To solve it they had two small, fragile ships, a double payload which was hopelessly inadequate, and six men. If the solution was to be as complete as possible, the abilities of the six men must cover the widest possible spread of physical and social science and, since the Ship was obviously the product of a highly advanced culture, the knowledge possessed by the six men should be complete and extensive.

Picking the men—six healthy, stable, intelligent men capable of surviving the longest journey in human history and asking the right questions at the end of it—was not an easy task because they had to choose men capable of collecting the bacon and bringing it home safely. Despite the thousands of scientifically eminent people who demanded to go on the trip, it was the space medics who had, as usual, the final say.

Instead of six of the world's acknowledged scientific geniuses, there had been chosen four experienced astronauts and two under training who were not even known in scientific circles, and respected only by a few friends. All that could be said for them was that they had a fairly good chance of surviving the trip.

McCullough, according to Berryman, had a subconscious which was dizzy from watching people go around in centrifuges, while Hollis, the supercargo in Morrison's ship, was a physicist working on the development of nuclear power plants for space vessels. All four of the astronauts had in their individual fashions told Hollis and McCullough that they approved of the choice which had been made—even though they may have been lying diplomatically—and that the two scientific unknowns should not worry about the things certain green-complexioned ivory tower types were saying about them. When they returned home they would all be as famous as anyone could hope to be.

Berryman cleared his throat loudly, bringing McCullough's mind back to present time with a rush as he said, "I suggest we do as the man said, Doctor —it's been thirty-one hours since we slept. Besides, it will still be there when you wake up."

"What will?" asked Walters.

"Nothing," said Berryman. "Millions of miles of nothing."

"I fell for that one," said Walters. He sighed and with great deliberation closed his eyes.

When they were quiet again waiting for the sedatives to work, McCullough's mind returned to the almost laughable problem of these people who insisted, quite wrongly, that they were his charges. He liked to think that his professional qualifications were necessary to the success of this trip, that he would spend his time making detailed observations and evaluating data gathered on extraterrestrial physiology, sociology, and even psychology although he was not himself a psychologist. But apart from five names, faces, tones of voice and military insignias, McCullough knew very little about his colleagues and self-elected patients.

Basically they were well adjusted introverts—an astronaut had no business being anything else—and both Captain Berryman and Major Walters had shown great thoughtfulness and consideration in their dealings with him.

Where Colonel Morrison was concerned he had less to go on. The colonel was polite but reserved and there had been very little prior social contact between them. The same applied to Major Drew. The third member of Morrison's crew was the physicist, Captain Hollis. His rank, like that of McCullough's, did not mean very much and had probably been given in order to simplify Army paperwork and make it easier for them to be ordered to do things. Hollis did not talk much and when he did it was in shy, low-voiced polysyllables. Apparently he got his kicks from playing chess and fixing his friends' TV sets.

Then there was Lieutenant Colonel McCullough, of course, a complex personality whose motivations McCullough had thought he understood until he found himself volunteering for this job. He had been undergoing training for MOL service, the idea being to have him share one of the orbiting laboratories with a number of lab animals and make a study of life processes in the weightless condition. Like the others he was unmarried and this was probably a good thing, despite the generally held belief that marriage gave added strength and emotional stability to an astronaut, because Prometheus might very well become a suicide mission.

McCullough wriggled in his couch even though all positions were equally comfortable in the weightless condition. Beyond the port, Earth was in darkness with the moon just about to slip over the sharply curved horizon. Cloud masses and continental outlines were gray and indistinct, with the stars above the horizon and the cities below it shining with the same intensity so that the whole planet seemed transparent and insubstantial, like a world of ectoplasm.

It was as if the final war had started and finished while he wasn't looking and the whole world had died, McCullough thought rather fancifully as he slipped over the edge of sleep, and a planet-sized ghost eternally pursued its orbit around the Sun . . .

But when he awakened some hours later, the Earth was again solid and condensed into a bright sphere which was just small enough to fit within the rim of the port. Berryman and Walters were already awake and when they saw that McCullough had joined them, the command pilot passed out breakfast. They were squeezing the last of it from their tubes when there was an interruption.

"This is Prometheus Control. Good morning, gentlemen! If you have nothing better to do, and we are sure you haven't, we would like you to take your first lecture. We have now decided to increase the frequency of these lectures from two to three per day. The first one, which should prove very helpful when you reach the Ship, deals with multidimensional geometry . . ."

"Ugh," said Berryman.

"Drop dead," said Walters.

"No comment," said McCullough.

"Thank you for your cooperation, gentlemen. If you will have pencils and paper ready . . ."

"Negative, negative!" the voice of Colonel Morrison broke in. *"P-One to Prometheus Control and P-Two. I advise against taking written notes. Paper is limited and may be needed for purposes of communications and supplementary sketches for the photographs taken at the Ship."*

"A good point, Colonel. Very well, mental notes only until a decision has been taken in this matter. And now, if you're ready to begin . . ."

There was a short silence broken by two bursts of static and an apologetic cough, then a new voice said, *"Well now, the subject of this lecture may itself need an explanation and it is this. From our observations of the approach, physical mass and general appearance of the alien ship, we are convinced that some method of faster-than-light propulsion is being used. Since Einsteinian math holds FTL travel to be impossible in this spacetime continuum we must fall back on those vaguer theories which suggest that the physical laws governing this continuum may be in some fashion sidestepped by traveling along or within some highly speculative hyperdimension. But as things stand you would very probably not know a hyperdimensional propulsion device if it stood up and bit you, and neither in all probability would I . . ."*

There was a small, dry, academic cough, then the voice went on, *"So the purpose of this lecture is, by outlining current thinking on this subject together with our speculations and supporting math, to give you a slightly better chance of recognizing a hyperdimensional generator if you should happen to see one.*

"Subsequent lectures on a wide range of subjects are expected to include . . ."

McCullough was beginning to feel concern for a future which now promised to be positively rather than negatively boring. He hoped the Prometheus people knew what they were doing and had taken pains to pick the right kind of lecturer. When the idea had been first mentioned they had agreed that without visual aids or textbooks the process of learning new and difficult subjects would be anything but easy. If handled properly the lectures would help negate boredom by engendering a competitive spirit among the two ships' crews. This would be a very good thing provided it did not cause some people to appear less bright than their fellows, a situation which could open the way to all sorts of conflicts and emotional disturbances. But all this had been taken into consideration, the Prometheus astronauts had been told, and any harmful side effects would be guarded against.

Probably time alone would tell, McCullough

thought. At least this lecturer possessed a rudimentary sense of humor.

He was saying, ". . . *To give you an example, our knowledge of extraterrestrial biology, physiology and sociology is nil. But in future lectures we will prepare you to a certain extent for whatever you may meet by considering in detail the sexual mores of certain isolated cultures on our own planet and the exotic reproductive mechanisms of our more alien terrestrial animals, insects and plants, and by formulating the type of social system these creatures might be expected to develop were they to rise to a human level of intelligence.*

"All this is simply an indication of what you may expect from the various specialist lecturers who will follow me.

"Before I commence my series of lectures it might be better if I introduced myself. I am Doctor— of Philosophy, not Medicine—Edward Ernest Pugh, Professor of Mathematics at the University of Coleraine, and Director of its Department of Extramural Studies . . ."

Berryman turned to stare very solemnly out of the Earth-side port. He said, "Just how extramural can a student get . . ."

Walters and McCullough laughed and Professor Pugh asked them to begin by considering a tesseract.

chapter three

TIME PASSED.

Their education grew while Earth and the apparent size of their vehicle shrank. When the bulkheads pressed in on them too closely they took turns going outside, treating incipient claustrophobia with threatened agoraphobia. At least that was how Berryman described the process. But he talked that way, as they all did, to hide his real feelings. The simple truth was that on the end of a long safety line, with their vehicle looking like some surrealistic toy five hundred yards away, the whole of Creation was spread out around them in sharp focus and perfect 3-D and it was not a sight which could be easily talked about.

With the increased distance from Earth and Prometheus Control, communication difficulties also grew. Not only did periodic solar interference make incoming messages barely intelligible, the time lag between outgoing questions and incoming answers was more than eight minutes. When it became necessary to turn up the gain on their receiver because a whisper of intelligence was trying to fight its way through a thunder of mush, the time lag was more than simply irritating. Finally even the colonel could stand it no longer.

"You may be transmitting a lecture on production methods in the aircraft industry," Morrison enunciated slowly and with sarcasm, *"but it sounds like a tape of Omaha Beach on D-Day. You are fighting a losing battle. Give up until these blasted sunspots have gone back to sleep, at least!"*

Eight minutes later a tiny voice fought its way through a barrage of static to say, *". . . Your message incompletely received . . . do not have battle tactics . . . Operation Overlord immediately available . . . loss to understand this request . . ."*

"You misunderstood my message, Prometheus Control," the colonel's voice returned, louder but with less clarity of diction. *"I requested that you cease transmission . . ."*

" . . . a lecture scheduled on Games Theory, but must warn you . . . Alien conception of military tactics may not agree . . . Eisenhower . . ."

"Don't talk when I'm interrupting, dammit. . . !"

For perhaps five minutes Control battled against the static with a complete lack of success, then the colonel's voice came again.

"P-One to P-Two. You may break contact with Control without their permission. I take full responsibility."

For a long time they simply luxuriated in the peace and quiet, then Walters said angrily, "You know, that noise was bad. You, sir, were practically tying yourself in knots and the doctor had his eyes squeezed shut and all his teeth showing. This is not good. Noise, any loud or unnecessary or unpleasant noise, especially in a confined space like this, makes me irritable. I'm beginning to dread these lectures three times a day. Somebody should do something about them. Somebody with authority!"

"I agree," said McCullough.

"Of course you agree!" Walters' voice was high-pitched, almost shrewish. "You always agree, but that's *all* you do. . . !"

"I think Morrison intends doing something," Berryman said quickly. He looked worriedly from Walters to McCullough and back, then went on. "And the doctor *is* a rather agreeable man, if a little hard to pin down at times. Myself, I expected him to look clinical occasionally and perhaps talk a bit dirty. At very least he should have spent a few days mentally dissecting us, explaining the real truth about our relationship with our first Teddy bear, and generally showing us what monstrous perverts we are under our warm, friendly exteriors. But he doesn't talk like a psychologist, or look like one or even admit to being one."

Berryman was trying hard to smooth things down and he was succeeding, but with his eyes he was asking the doctor for a little help.

"Well now," said McCullough gravely, "you must understand first that, if anything, I would be an Eysenckian rather than a Freudian psychologist and so would never have had an occasion to use a couch professionally. But there was one period when I did some valuable research if I do say so myself, on the behavior and psychology of worms.

"There were some quite intriguing incidents," McCullough went on. "They had numbers instead of names, so there is no question of an unethical disclosure of privileged information, and they had such a low order of intelligence that to get through to them at all we had to stimulate the clitellum with a mild electric . . ."

Berryman shook his head.

"Well, I did try," said McCullough, projecting a hurt expression. He went on, "As for making noises like a psychologist and pushing your mental buttons, this would be a waste of time. You are both well adjusted, self-aware, intellectually and emotionally honest and already well versed in the terminology, so that any problem which arises is immediately recognized, classified and dealt with by the person concerned. So there isn't anything for me to do even if I was supposed to do it."

For perhaps a minute there was silence, then Walters said, "I'm sorry I blew up at you, Doctor. If I'd been using my head at all I should have realized that anyone who turns nasty with a psychologist ends up being flattered to death."

"My point exactly!" said McCullough to Berryman. "He can even see through my subtle attempts at manipulation by flattery!"

Berryman nodded and said, "Now if only the aliens on the Ship are worms . . ."

The crew of P-Two were back to normal.

But on a wider, more objective level the situation was definitely not normal. The space inside P-Two not taken up with control, communications and life-support systems, left very little room for either movement or privacy. Their total living space was a hollow cylinder seven feet in diameter and four deep, and this was further reduced by couches, control consoles and instrumentation which projected into it. Nobody could move more than a few inches without sticking an elbow or a knee in someone's face or stomach. Even the sanitary arrangements gave visual privacy only. And because their tanked oxygen was restricted, trips outside the ship were kept down to a total of two hours per week, and they just could not be alone for the length of time required by normal introverts. Instead they lay strapped loosely into their couches for an hour or so each day, pitting one muscle against another, talking or not talking, listening to incoming signals and smelling to high heaven.

In living quarters which compared unfavorably with the most unenlightened penal institutions, the crew of P-Two—and P-One, presumably—shared a not always peaceful coexistence. They tried to be polite and considerate to each other, but not too much so. The effort of guarding one's tongue continually, of *always* being polite, would have been so much of a strain that the emotional backlash would have led inevitably to violence.

Instead they were normally bad-tempered or sarcastic, while remaining at all times sensitive to potentially dangerous changes of atmosphere. If they sensed that the subject of their displeasure or sarcasm was becoming too strongly affected by it, the remarks were allowed to grow to ridiculous and laughable proportions. They became adepts at walking this psychological tightrope. But they were subject to severe external pressures as well.

Earth had decided to investigate the Ship with a group of trained astronauts rather than a cross-section of the best scientific brains, and all things considered it had been a sound decision. But Earth desperately wanted things to go right at the Ship. They wanted a smooth social and cultural contact and they badly wanted to find out everything they possibly could about alien science and technology. As a result, they were trying to cover themselves both ways by doing everything possible to make scientific investigators out of their astronauts.

The low signal to noise ratio during some of the lectures was merely an added irritant. The real trouble was that the lectures themselves were a constant reminder to every one of them of what lay at the end of the trip.

Any well adjusted person could face up to a problem once it was defined. But when nothing at all was known about it other than that it is in the life-and-death category and that it *must* somehow be solved, even the sanest personality could show signs of strain.

They were now three weeks away in time from the alien Ship . . .

After one lecture so speculative that it was almost pure science fiction, Walters said, "It would be nice if we could simply hold our hands out in the universal gesture of peace. But what *is* the universal gesture of peace to an octopus or an intelligent vegetable?"

McCullough said, "We don't usually make gestures of peace at animals or vegetables, so their gestures toward us are either defensive or hostile. Tortoises retreat under their shells, octopuses squirt ink at us, and plants grow thorns if they are able. Offhand I'd say that if an animal or being behaves normally when it is approached by a stranger—that is, if it doesn't take any offensive or defensive action—then it is either peacefully inclined, or suffering from an impairment of sensory equipment or brainpower. But this is an unsatisfactory answer, since it may involve a being whose normal reactions will be just as strange to us as its abnormal ones. I don't know."

"Let us suppose," Berryman said, "that the Ship

is solidly packed with a vitamin-enriched sandy substance—except for certain hollowed-out areas for
power and control systems—with provision made for
renewing the food element and eliminating wastes.
Furniture, bedding and so on would be virtually
nonexistent, and control levers and—and push pads
they would have to be, rather than push buttons—
would be positioned all the way around and perhaps
inside the mechanism they were designed to control.
This being would curl itself around and insinuate
itself into the machine it was operating . . ."

"Not worms again," said Walters.

"I'm talking about an intelligent, wormlike life-
form," the Command Pilot went on. "A worm who
stayed out of its burrow long enough to look up and
wonder at the stars . . ."

"Oh, very poetic," said Walters.

"Shuddup you . . . A worm who developed intelligence and the degree of cooperation which made
possible civilization and technological progress. And
now, Doctor, suppose you were confronted by a
member of such a species. With your specialist
knowledge of the physiology and motivations of
what amounts to the aboriginal ancestors of these
beings, could you arrive at an understanding with
them?"

McCullough thought for a moment, then said, "An
analogy would be an alien able to understand a
human being from data gained while examining a
baboon. I don't think it is possible. In any case the
intellectual and evolutionary gap between your star-
traveling worms and mine is much greater than that
between a man and a baboon. This is why we are
being subjected to these lectures on the mating habits
of armadillos and things . . ."

"Things, he says." Berryman made a face and began passing out lunch.

They nearly always ate after a discussion about the beings on the Ship, but Berryman and Walters had stopped mentioning the psychological connection between feelings of insecurity and eating. The only person to speak at all during the meal was Walters, who said thoughtfully, "You know, Doctor, there must be *something* you can do!"

Three days later something came up which the doctor *could* do. Something, apparently, which *only* the doctor could do.

"Morrison here. Put the doctor on, please."

"Yes, sir," said McCullough.

"Captain Hollis is having trouble. A—a skin condition, among other things. He won't sleep without heavy sedation and we're running out of that. I realize it is a lot to ask, but I'd prefer you to see him rather than prescribe from where you are. Can you come over to P-One, Doctor?"

Instinctively McCullough looked out at the stars. He could not see P-One because it was visible only on the radar screen. The last time anyone had seen it was when they were being inserted into orbit above Earth. He cleared his throat and said, "Yes, of course."

"At this distance there is an element of risk involved."

"I realize that."

"Very well. Thank you."

When the colonel had signed off, Walters gave McCullough a long, steady look, then held up three fingers. He said, "One, you're stupid. Two, you're brave. Or three, you've been brainwashed."

chapter four

THE PERSONNEL LAUNCHER was a light-alloy rigid pipe fifty feet long, built up in sections and slotted together without projections of any kind. It was assembled forward so as to form a continuation of the center line of the ship, and the charge which tossed its human missile into space was matched by an equal thrust directed aft so as to avoid the necessity of course corrections. On this occasion the whole ship had to be aimed at the target on a radar bearing rather than a visual sighting.

Berryman threaded the launching harness onto the first section of pipe and, while Walters completed the erection, the command pilot harnessed McCullough to the stupid contraption. It was a little odd that McCullough regarded it as a contraption now, when on Earth, after studying drawings and operating principles and seeing the demonstration films, he had considered it an ingenious and foolproof device.

The harness itself was a somewhat lopsided fabrication of thin metal tubing built around the hol-

23

low cylinder which fitted over the launching pipe, with the bulky oxygen and reaction tanks grouped on one side and the body webbing on the other. But when a man was attached to the harness with his arms drawn back and joined behind him and his legs bent vertically at the knees—there were special cuffs and stirrups fitted so that this could be done comfortably—the device began to assume a degree of symmetry. With the man added the center of thrust roughly coincided with the center of gravity so that the system had only a slight tendency to spin after launching.

"The push will send you off at just under fifteen miles per hour," Berryman told McCullough for the third or fourth time, "so if our shooting is very good and you hit P-One at this speed, it would be like running into a brick wall. You would hurt yourself, you might damage or rupture your suit and the impact could wreck the other ship . . ."

"Don't joke about things like that, Berryman! Besides, you'll make him nervous."

"I wasn't joking, Colonel," the command pilot replied. Then to McCullough he went on, "I was trying to make you cautious rather than nervous, Doctor. Just remember to check your velocity with respect to the other ship in plenty of time. Start decelerating when you are about a mile off, come to a stop not too close, then edge in on your gas motor. You have a good reserve of reaction mass, your air will last for six hours, and the trip will take roughly three and a half hours since P-One is over fifty miles away . . ."

"Suppose it isn't there after three and a half hours?" said McCullough. "It's a very small ship and . . ."

"Such morbid imaginings," said Walters severely, "ill behove a psychological gentleman . . ."

"You're ready to go, Doctor," said Berryman. "Give me ten minutes to get inside and check the radar bearing again. Walters, keep clear of the launcher . . ."

The launch itself was an anticlimax: just a comfortable, solid push that reminded McCullough of the first few seconds in an express elevator. Then he cleared the guide tube and was tumbling very slowly end over end.

Quickly he withdrew his arms and legs from their retaining clips and, when P-Two came into sight again, spread them out to check his spin. Walters and Berryman did not talk, although he could hear the sound of their breathing in his phones, and McCullough kept silent as well. The ship dwindled in size very slowly—it did not appear to move away from him, just to grow smaller—so that the launcher was dismantled and the tiny figures of the two pilots had re-entered the lock before distance made the finer details of the vehicle run together into a silvery triangular blur.

Just before it disappeared completely, McCullough rotated himself until he was facing his direction of travel, and began searching for an identical blur which would be Morrison's ship, even though the soonest he could hope to see it would be in another two hours.

The colonel had suggested that he sleep on the way over, leaving his receiver switched on at full volume so that Morrison could wake him when it became necessary. McCullough had refused this suggestion for two reasons. The one he gave the colonel was that he did not want to be half asleep when he closed with P-One—making contact might be a tricky enough job with him wide-awake. The other reason he did not tell anyone. It was his fear of waking up with no ship in sight, beyond all help or hope of help, alone . . .

He was very much aware of the safety line coiled neatly at his waist, and of the fact that the other end of it was not attached to anything.

But that was just the beginning . . .

In the weightless condition no muscular effort was required to keep arms and legs outstretched, and in that attitude spin was reduced to a minimum. But gradually the position began to feel awkward and ridiculous and, in some obscure fashion, unprotected. All around him the stars hung bright and close and beautiful, but the blackness between them went on and on forever. He told himself truthfully that he enjoyed being out here, that there was nothing to threaten him, nothing to be immediately afraid of, and nobody to see his fear even if he should show it.

He was all alone.

His rate of spin began to increase slowly, then rapidly as his outstretched arms and legs contracted until his knees were drawn up against his stomach and his arms, with the elbows tucked in as far as his suit would allow, folded tightly across his chest. But it was not until he realized that his eyes were squeezed shut that McCullough began to wonder what exactly it was that was happening to him.

He badly needed to straighten himself out, in both senses of the word.

But for some odd reason his body had passed beyond the control of his mind, just as the various layers of his mind were no longer under the control of his will. He was feeling rather than thinking. It was as if he were an enormous, dry sponge soaking up, saturating itself in loneliness—the purely subjective loneliness of being unknown and unnoticed in a crowd, the actual loneliness of being on a deserted beach where the uncaring natural phenomena of wind and wave press all around, and the awful, lost feeling of the child in the night who believes, whether rightly or wrongly, that he is unwanted and unloved. The feeling which was welling up inside McCullough was loneliness distilled, concentrated and ultimately refined. Anything in his previous experience was like comparing a slight overexposure to the sun with third-degree burns.

He crouched into himself even more tightly while the unseen stars whirled around him and the hot tears forced their way between his squeezed-together lids.

Then the awful feeling of loneliness began to withdraw, or perhaps he was withdrawing from it. The weightless spinning was oddly pleasant. There was a timeless, hypnotic quality about it. The sensation was like the moment after a tumble into deep water when it is impossible to tell if one is upside down or not, and yet the warm salt water is supporting and protecting and pressing close . . .

"*Say* something!" shouted McCullough.

"Something," said Berryman promptly.

"*Anything wrong, Doctor?*"

"Not—not really, sir," said McCullough. "Whatever it was—I'm all right now."

"*Good! I thought you were sleeping after all—you haven't made a sound for over two hours. We should be just about visible to you now.*"

McCullough straightened and slowed his spin. The stars rose majestically above the upper rim of his visor, reached zenith and then slowly set between his feet. When the sun came around he covered it with his hand so as not to be blinded, and he searched the sky. But the two bright objects he picked out were too brilliant to be P-One—they were probably Sirius and Jupiter, but he was so disoriented that he could not be sure.

"I can't find you."

There must have been an edge of panic in his tone because Morrison said quickly, *"You're doing fine, Doctor. Our radar shows a solid trace for P-Two. If you were off course to any large extent there would be two traces, so any divergence is minor. Look around you, carefully."*

Perhaps ten minutes went by, then Morrison said, *"When you were launched, our position with respect to your ship was approximately ten degrees below and fifteen degrees to the right of the central star in the right half of the W in Cassiopeia, or above and to the left of the left center star if you're turned around and it looks like an M. Use Cassiopeia as your center and search outward into Perseus, Andromeda and Cepheus—do you get the idea? The closer you are to us the greater will be our apparent displacement.*

"We should be the brightest object in sight by now. You should begin deceleration in seven and one half minutes . . ."

And if he did not decelerate, McCullough would go past P-One, possibly without even seeing it. But if he decelerated without seeing it and directing his thrust in the right section of sky, the chances were that he would go off at a tangent or shoot past the ship at double his present velocity. If that happened, he doubted very much whether his air or his reaction mass would be sufficient for him to find his way back.

McCullough tried not to pursue that line of thought. He tried so hard that before he realized it, his knees were drawn up and his arms pressed tightly against his chest again, and the stars were swirling around him like a jeweled blizzard. He swore suddenly and starfished again, forcing his mind to concentrate on the slowly wheeling heavens so that he could impose some sort of order out of what had become a mass of tiny, unidentifiable lights. He viewed them with his head straight and tilted to each side, or he tried to imagine them upside down, and gradually he was able to see them with the imaginary lines connecting one to the other, which gave them the shapes of Hunters and Archers and Crabs. He realized suddenly that as well as spinning head over heels he had also been turning sideways, and he was able to identify Capella, which was hanging out beyond his left hip.

Capella had picked up a very strange companion.

As quickly as possible, McCullough lined himself up on the object, placed hands and feet into the cuffs and stirrups, then said, "I have you. Standing by to decelerate."

"In eight seconds, Doctor. And I must say you cut it close ... Now!"

A little later Morrison said, *"We can see your gas discharge, Doctor. Very nice shooting, P-Two."*

From the other ship there came sounds of Berryman and Walters being modest. McCullough's precalculated period of deceleration ceased, leaving him barely three hundred yards from the other ship, where two tiny figures were already crawling out of the airlock and onto the hull. He aimed himself carefully and jetted slowly toward them.

Morrison said, *"As you know, Doctor, there is no privacy and very little space for a physical examination in the control module, so Drew and I will erect the launcher for your return while you have a look at Captain Hollis. Take your time—within reason, of course—and signal with the airlock lamp when you've finished. You may not want us to be listening with our suit radios . . ."*

There was little conversation after that until McCullough made contact with the hull and negotiated the airlock. He found himself in a control module which was in every respect identical to the one on the other ship—it even smelled as bad—and differed only in the figure occupying the supernumary's position.

McCullough gave Hollis a long, sympathetic, clinical look and then sighed. Unoriginally he said, "What seems to be the trouble?"

chapter five

It was a simple question but McCullough knew the answer would be a complicated one. Hollis was a distressed and deeply troubled man.

There was, of course, no provision for taking baths on the Prometheus expedition, but the crews had periodic alcohol rubdowns to unclog their pores, the alcohol being filtered out and reclaimed by the air circulation system. While their meals lacked bulk, they contained all the necessary vitamins. Even so, as McCullough peeled the one-piece coverall from Hollis' shoulders and arms he could not help thinking about ancient sailing ships with water going green in their casks and the crews down with scurvy or worse . . .

A large area of the physicist's body had obviously not known the alcohol pad for months—the skin was clogged and dry and scaling—and his arms, chest and shoulders were covered with raw patches and sores, the condition extending up to his face and neck. Despite having no fingernails to speak of, it was plain that Hollis had been continually picking or rubbing at them through his coveralls until his body must have become one great, livid itch.

"Can you remember when this trouble started?" McCullough asked quietly, trying to ignore the pricklings of the sympathetic itch that was creeping over his own body.

"About—about nine weeks out," Hollis answered. His eyes would not meet McCullough's and his hands twitched and crawled all over his body. He went on, "I suppose it started about two weeks after Drew let slip—after I found out what they were doing. But I can't tell you about that."

"Why not?" said McCullough, smiling. "I don't shock very easily, you know."

Hollis looked startled and for a moment he almost laughed, then he said quickly, apologetically, "I'm sorry, I gave you the wrong impression. It isn't shocking like that. They—they have a secret. They *do* have a secret! Of course they don't know I know about it. Walters and Berryman aren't in on it, either. Or you. But it's bad. You've no idea how bad. But I'm sorry—I can't tell you about it, I don't know how you'd react. You might let something slip to Morrison. Or you might blow the whole thing wide open and be a party to . . . I suppose it would be mutiny. I'm sorry, it wouldn't be fair to burden you with this thing. I—I don't want to talk about it."

But it was quite obvious that he did want to talk about it, desperately, and that McCullough would have very little coaxing to do to have this deep, dark, desperate secret revealed to him in its entirety. He said, still smiling, "I expect you know best. But it would have been nice to take back a juicy piece of gossip to the other ship . . ."

"This is serious, damn you!"

"Very well," McCullough said, less pleasantly. "Your present condition is something we *will* have to talk about. And because I prefer the talk to be private, and Morrison and Drew have a limited supply of air out there, we will have to cut a few corners.

"Since *everyone* on this expedition seems to be very well informed on the subjects of psychiatry and psychology," he went on, smiling again, "I'll assume that you have a fair understanding of the operation of the subconscious mind. You will be aware of the perfectly normal pressures, conflicts of personality and basic insecurities to which all of us are subject, also of the fact that these are seriously aggravated by our present environment. This being so, you must realize that your physical trouble, this unsightly and uncomfortable skin condition, has a purely psychological basis. There are no germs, no vitamin deficiencies, nothing to which you would be allergic on the ship."

If Berryman and Walters could hear me now, McCullough thought briefly. The trouble was it was so easy to *talk* like a psychologist . . .

He went on, "Well now, I realize that being separated from the rest of humanity by fifty million miles is bad enough. But if you have been rejected, or feel that you have been rejected by the other men in the ship, that could be the initial cause of your trouble. Your evident anxiety over this secret you have uncovered will not have helped matters."

McCullough had an almost overwhelming urge to scratch his left armpit through his spacesuit, and another sympathetic itch raged behind his right knee. He continued, "A rejected person tends to become self-conscious and much more aware of himself both physically and mentally. Your body becomes much more sensitive, even hypersensitive, to stimuli which are normally ignored. Your trouble probably began with an itchy scalp or ear lobe which you scratched almost without thinking. But gradually, through constant repetition and irritation, the psychosomatic itch became a real one.

"This is an extreme oversimplification, of course," McCullough said. "Doubtless there were many other factors which contributed to your present sorry state. But right now we should do something positive about alleviating your present condition—with something more than lanolin since that would relieve only the physical symptoms. Also, since the axiom that a trouble shared is a trouble halved is so old and true that it was used before psychology was invented, I would like to know what the other two are keeping secret which distresses you so much. I'll be discreet, of course . . ."

He let the sentence hang, but obviously Hollis needed more coaxing. McCullough tried a different tack. He said, "What is Morrison like as a person? And Drew? How have their relations toward you changed since the beginning of the trip? Be as objective as you can . . ."

A person could say an awful lot about themselves by the way they talked about someone else.

As he began to talk, Hollis may have thought that he was being objective, and McCullough, too, lost quite a lot of his objectivity as he listened. He began to feel angry with Morrison and Drew, particularly with the colonel. For despite his phenomenal brain,

Hollis had always been the shy, timid, eager-to-please type and the necessary allowances should have been made. As his relations with the other two had steadily worsened, in an attempt to get on better terms with them again, his timidity had increased to ridiculous and quite irritating proportions for a grown man. He had abased himself and fawned and generally carried on like a frightened dog.

This was not the way Hollis told it, of course. McCullough was reading between the lines.

It had started because the colonel and Drew knew each other long before either of them were connected with astronautics. They had served together briefly in southeast Asia and Drew had done Morrison some sort of favor. Hollis had been unable to ascertain whether the favor had been sordid or sublime, whether it involved white slavery, the black market of just saving the colonel's life.

As the weeks went by, the two had talked together more and more often about their small war, mentioning people and places and making stupid, in-group jokes. Hollis was excluded to an increasing extent from these conversations and when, out of sheer desperation, he tried to join in, he usually made a mess of it and stopped the conversation stone dead.

Listening to the physicist, McCullough could not help thinking of his own ship. He hesitated to make comparisons with the two comedian-psychologists on P-Two, and the sometimes artificial atmosphere of good cheer they generated, but if Morrison and Drew had made a similar effort, Hollis would probably not be in his present condition. From his knowledge of Hollis during training, he thought the physicist, once he got over his initial shyness and timidity, would have been a very pleasant and stimulating person to have on a long voyage.

Instead they had talked about their jungle air war as if it had been some kind of exclusive holiday, in a language which excluded Hollis. Then they had gone on to talk about another matter—again in the cryptic, slangy manner the physicist was not supposed to understand. But Hollis had been able to understand —a little at first, then later he had been able to piece together the whole frightful operation. He freely admitted to McCullough that he was uneducated where such things as women and power politics were concerned, because so much of his life had been spent in collecting degrees, but this did not mean that he was stupid. . . !

"This was when you became restless and itchy, I take it," McCullough broke in at that point, "and you began to irritate the others. How did they react?"

"The colonel didn't react at all," said Hollis. "He just looked long-suffering and stopped talking to me completely. Drew swore at me for a time, then he went the same way. They started going outside together between lectures, connecting their air lines to the ship supply so as not to waste tanked air. They switched off their radios sometimes and talked by touching helmets. But there was sound conduction along the return air line and sometimes I could make out a word here and there. Enough to know what was going on.

"Did you know," Hollis rushed on, "that the Hold at takeoff was deliberate? That Morrison has made no attempt to close the distance between the two expendable, did you know that? They've discussed all sorts of hypothetical approaches and tactics to use ships? Fuel conservation, he says—but your ship is against the alien ship, the desirability of an armed as opposed to an unarmed approach . . ."

Hollis' arms were partly folded and he was tearing absent-mindedly at his forearms with fingernails which had been gnawed too short to do any real damage. Suddenly he stopped scratching, closed his eyes tightly and said, "I'm sorry. I didn't want to tell you. But you've a right to know, Doctor. P-One is carrying a Dirty Annie!"

Dirty Annie was a nuclear device which was a little too destructive and long-lasting in its aftereffects to be called tactical. McCullough was silent for a moment as he thought over all the implications of what he had heard, then he said, "This is serious."

It was a dangerously ambiguous remark, he realized as soon as he said it, but Hollis had not noticed that. The physicist was talking furiously, apologizing for sharing his worries with the doctor, pleading with him not to tell the colonel, and to *do* something about Morrison and Drew. McCullough listened with half his mind while the other half cringed with sympathy.

Not all of the sympathy was for Hollis.

Morrison and Drew could not have had a very pleasant time either, driven as they had been into long periods of unscheduled extravehicular activity. They may well have been guilty of thoughtlessness in their dealings with Hollis, but constant EVA put a dangerous strain on their suits. The P-Ships could not afford the weight penalty of carrying spare spacesuits, much less weaponry.

McCullough wondered suddenly what shape his own delusion would have taken, what particular nightmare his own subconscious would have dredged up, if Walters and Berryman had rejected him. An atomic bomb was perhaps a too simple form for a physicist's nightmare to take, but then at heart Hollis was a very simple man.

There still remained the question of his treatment.

Very quietly and seriously McCullough said, "Naturally I shall not mention this to the colonel or Drew. At the proper time I may discuss it with Walters and Berryman—but they won't talk out of turn either. It's hard to say exactly what we must do about it until the time comes, but when it does, remember that we will be four against their two. And remember this as well; the problem isn't yours alone any more—three of your friends will be helping you solve it. They may even, since they are not so close to it as you are and may thus be able to consider the problem more objectively, solve it for you. Think about this, won't you? Think about it really hard."

McCullough paused for a moment, then went on, "You have already realized that your condition is directly attributable to worry about this bomb—anyone with an ounce of sensitivity in them would have reacted in much the same fashion. But there is no necessity to worry now—at least to the extent where it affects you physically.

"You may be surprised how quickly this skin condition clears up," he continued, "and how comfortable you will begin to feel generally. The colonel will be surprised, too, and for that reason I'll leave a supply of medication to help the process along. Morrison will assume that the salve and tablets are effecting a cure, but this is a necessary subterfuge since you can't very well tell him the real cause of your improvement—the fact that his secret is now common property. But in order to allay his suspicions further, I will have to be very tough—or appear to be very tough—on you."

McCullough was going to be very tough with Drew and the colonel as well. He was going to insist that Morrison pad and bandage the patient's hands so that he would be unable to scratch himself, giving his skin condition a chance to heal, which meant that Hollis would have to be fed and generally wet-nursed by the other two men. Drew would probably come in for most of the work, but the application of salve and the checking of Hollis' condition—McCullough would insist on daily progress reports—would be a two-man job. In short, Hollis must no longer be treated as an outcast, and Morrison and Drew would be made to realize that psychosomatic leprosy was not catching.

Drew and the colonel might not be too gentle in their treatment of the patient at first, it would be embarrassing for all concerned and the atmosphere would be anything but warm and friendly. But at least they would not be ignoring Hollis and that was an important first step. Later, other steps would suggest themselves. McCullough was confident that it would be only a matter of time before the physicist was back to normal and the relationships inside P-One more—harmonious.

At no time did McCullough consider the possibility of the colonel refusing to cooperate. In the medical area Morrison was outranked and he was not the type to disobey a lawful order.

Later, when they were all crammed into the control module, McCullough was relieved and pleased at the reception given his suggestions for treating Hollis. It was now apparent that the other two had felt a

certain amount of guilt over the way they had behaved toward the physicist and were very anxious to
make it up to him. It restored McCullough's faith in
people, especially in cold, withdrawn and not very
friendly people like Morrison and Drew. He would
have liked a long, private talk with the two men as
well, if only to get their side of the business, but in
the circumstances that might not be possible without
running the risk of having Hollis think he had acquired another enemy instead of three friends . . .

He had a lot to think about on the way back, and
this time he kept his hands and feet in their cuffs and
stirrups and his eyes wide open until he saw P-Two
again and Berryman and Walters were helping him
out of his suit and he was saying, in a tone much
more serious than he had intended, "It's nice to be
home again."

chapter six

RADIO INTERFERENCE HAD all but disappeared so
that the lectures, music, last-minute instructions and
reminders that this was an epoch-making event and
would they please not do anything silly, poured in
on them constantly and so clearly that they had no
real excuse to switch off. They were told that they
must at all costs remember and apply the knowledge
gained during their trip out, but at the same time
they must not hesitate to forget all of their scientific,
sociological and psychological theories and precon-
ceptions if the situation warranted it. They were told
to do, or not do, this several times an hour.

One did not have to be a psychologist to realize
that the people at Prometheus Control had worked
themselves into a fine state of jitters.

"The awful black immensity of space," said Walters sourly during one of the rare radio silences.
"The vast and aching loneliness between the stars,
the unutterable, soul-destroying boredom. Dammit,

they won't even give us ten minutes peace and quiet to feel bored *in*."

Shaking his head, Berryman intoned, "Is some superhuman extraterrestrial intelligence already brushing our minds with unfelt tendrils of thought, sizing us up, judging us and perhaps with us the whole human race? Or is some bug-eyed bugger sitting at a rocket launcher just waiting for us to come into range?"

"We've been over all this before!" said McCullough, suddenly angry at the pilot for bringing up the subject which they all wanted to leave alone. Then awkwardly he tried to turn it into a joke by adding, "Three times in the last hour . . ."

"Thrust in minus thirty seconds, P-Two. Stand by, P-One . . ."

There was a note of self-satisfaction overlaying the tension in the voice of Control and, considering the fact that their computations had resulted in them hitting an impossibly small target with both ships, their smugness was perhaps justified. But McCullough wondered, a little cynically, how pleased an arrow was with the archer when a bull's-eye or a miss into the sandbags would result in an equally violent headache . . .

Deceleration was a strangely uncomfortable sensation after so many months' weightlessness. On Morrison's ship, thrust was delayed by several seconds to allow P-One to draw closer to P-Two—but not too close. It had been decided that Berryman's ship would approach the alien vessel directly to within a distance of one mile, with the command pilot reporting back every yard of the way and using his initiative if something untoward occurred. With P-One's more powerful transmitter Morrison would relay these reports back to Control, advising Berryman if or when necessary, and Control would do nothing but listen.

Because of the radio time lag, anything they might say would come too late to be useful.

All decisions on procedure in the area of the alien ship were thus the responsibility of Colonel Morrison. Berryman could exercise a little initiative to begin with, but once the situation was evaluated, all major decisions would be taken by the colonel. As a precautionary measure the thrust and attitude of P-One had been modified so as to bring it to a stop fifty miles short of the alien ship.

McCullough wondered what Hollis was making of *that*.

In the three weeks since he had visited him, the physicist's condition, both physical and mental, had improved enormously. Hollis had spoken to him several times and had said so—without, of course, mentioning the Dirty Annie business. McCullough was well aware that Hollis could not, by any stretch of the imagination, be said to have been cured, but at least his condition had improved to the point where his difficulties, both emotional and physical, no longer impaired his functioning—and that was half the battle.

On the radar screen the target showed as a pulsing blob of light which crept steadily down the distance scale, and in the telescope the Ship grew and spread until it overflowed the field of view. Gradually P-Two's velocity with respect to the other vessel lessened until it hung motionless at a distance of one mile from the Ship.

Like a minnow investigating a sleeping shark, McCullough thought.

Berryman cleared his throat loudly and said, "The—the Ship is broadside on to us. I estimate its length at just under half a mile and its diameter at about one hundred yards. The diameter is uniform throughout its length, like a torpedo, except where it curves inward at nose and stern. Two-thirds of the way toward the stern—I'm assuming it is the stern because the other end contains more transparent material—the hull is encircled by a belt of large, transparent blisters. Twelve of them, I think. The sun is shining directly into one and I can see metallic reflections.

"There is another cluster of transparent domes encircling the nose," he went on, "but these are smaller and flatter—possibly housing the Ship's communications and sensory equipment, while the bigger ones are either weapons or—or ... Maybe Professor Pugh would have some ideas on what they are, because there is nothing visible on the Ship resembling a conventional rocket motor or even a jet orifice ..."

The pilot was dividing his attention between the telescope and the direct vision port. His voice was quiet, controlled and ostentatiously matter-of-fact. But every time he moved, the perspiration beading his forehead was shaken loose and hung suspended away from his face, like the stylized sweat of startlement of a character in a comic strip. Walters' lower lip had disappeared behind his upper teeth and McCullough did not know how he himself looked, but he did not feel at all well.

Berryman went on steadily, "We are beaming signal patterns denoting, we hope, intelligence at them on a wide spread of frequencies and we are igniting flares every fifteen minutes. So far there has been no response. I don't understand this—we're not exactly sneaking up on them. Have I permission to move in?"

To give him credit, Morrison did not warn them to be careful or remind them, again, of the absolute necessity of doing the right thing. Instead he said, *"Very well. We will close to one mile and cover you . . ."*

"What with?" said McCullough, in spite of himself.

He had been thinking about Hollis again and the physicist's delusion about a Dirty Annie on P-One. McCullough wondered suddenly if such delusions were contagious, like some kind of psychosomatic head cold . . .

"A figure of speech, Doctor. We shall furnish moral support only. And please remember that everything we say is being rebroadcast all over Earth, so keep this channel clear for Captain Berryman."

For the past few minutes McCullough had completely forgotten that everything emanating from P-Two was being relayed through Prometheus Control all over the world. He could just imagine the battery of ground-bound space medics playing back that section of their tape, discussing each word and inflection in the minutest possible detail and muttering among themselves about father figures and archetypal images and basic insecurities. McCullough felt his face beginning to burn, but the two pilots were too busy repositioning their ship to notice it.

For the better part of their arbitrary 'day' they drifted slowly back and forth along the tremendous alien hull. Each pass covered a different strip of its surface, allowing them to chart the various features it contained. When they approached the transparant domes in what they assumed was the bows, they lit a flare, but there was no reaction, no sign of life of any kind.

Berryman said, "Either there is nobody at home or the watch-keeping officer is asleep or worse. If it wasn't for the fact that the Ship decelerated into a circumsolar orbit, and a very neat one at that, I'd say there was a strong possibility that the Ship is in a derelict or at least distressed condition . . ."

"A ship in distress usually signals for help. As loudly and as often as possible."

"If they were telepathic," said McCullough, joining in, "they might expect their distress to be plain for all to hear."

"If they were telepathic they would know that we weren't."

Berryman shot the doctor a brief, sympathetic glance, then went on quickly, "They can't or won't react to the usual methods of attracting attention and their ship appears to be in a powered-down condition. I think it is time we knocked on the nearest airlock door and walked in—politely, of course, and with all due caution.

"I suggest leaving the doctor on watch," Berryman went on, "while Walters and I have a look at the big seal which is passing under us just now. It looks like a cargo lock big enough to take P-Two from here, and there is a smaller lock—for personnel, I expect—set into the large one. I think we could open it. After all, there are only so many ways to open a door . . ."

Morrison was silent for so long that they wondered if he was going to wait for instructions from Earth before giving permission. But finally he said, *"I agree that we should take some more positive action, but I'm concerned about the possibility of booby traps. Unintentional booby traps in the shape of mechanisms whose operating principles are so alien as to be a danger to you."*

"We'll be careful, sir," said Berryman.

"We're only going to open a door," Walters whispered disparagingly to the doctor, but not quietly enough.

"Pandora thought the same thing, Walters, you might remember that! However, you have permission to land on the Ship's hull and open an airlock. Take your time about preparations—there must be no avoidable accidents. And you, Berryman, will remain on watch. I can't risk losing both pilots, Walters and the doctor can go—if they don't mind, that is . . ."

Put like that and with countless millions listening, they had, of course, no choice.

But the strange thing was that McCullough did not feel afraid—tense and impatient with all the waiting around, perhaps, but not really afraid. Earlier, when they had been approaching the Ship for the first time, he had been expecting literally anything and he had been more afraid than he had believed it possible for any man to be. Perhaps it had been what some people called a moment of truth. But when the moment of truth spreads itself out over twenty-six hours, there is a considerable dilution of effect.

McCullough launched himself in the wake of the pilot, slowly and carefully so that his magnets would stick to the alien hull rather than bounce off, and a few minutes later they made a gentle, sprawling contact. McCullough detached his wrist magnets and slowly straightened up.

It was only then that it hit him.

This metal plating beneath his feet had been shaped and processed from ore dug out of the earth, but not *the* Earth. From his position by the airlock the hull looked so enormous that he seemed almost to be standing on a metallic planet complete with a range of beautiful transparent hills. The sun was shining through one of the blister hills, distorted by refraction into a gaudy smear which threw blurred highlights off whatever it was that the blister contained. And this whole vast fabrication was the product of a design staff and engineers who were not of Earth. At no stage in its construction had the people from McDonnell or BAC had a single thing to do with it.

Its reason for being might be as strange and alien as its makers, whoever and whatever they might be, but McCullough felt that its basic purpose could be easily understood by human beings of a certain psychological type—the type who drowned or crashed or fell off mountains trying to climb higher or fly faster or dive deeper than their fellows.

For some reason McCullough felt sure that the aliens had gone to the stars, had come to *this* star, simply because it was there . . .

"When they were giving us all those lectures, Doctor," said Walters, displaying his genius for converting the sublime into the ridiculous, "they forgot Burglary. How *does* one pick an airlock?"

chapter seven

THERE ARE ONLY so many ways for a door to open," Walters said, very seriously for him, "and I'd like you to check me on them. It can be hinged to open inward or out. It can slide open by moving up, down or to either side. It can be mounted on a central pivot, like a butterfly valve, or it can unscrew. Have I left anything out?"

"I don't think so," said McCullough. "But if these people were advanced enough to have molecular engineering, the entrances might iris open and shut . . ."

"Unlikely," said Walters. "The door and surround are ordinary metal, very roughly finished and showing deep scratches and dents. If they were capable of controlling the molecular binding forces of metal to the extent of being able to dilate an opening in an area of solid plating—of making the mental flow like a viscous liquid—they would not have scratches showing on it. These markings could have been made by heavy tools or equipment being moved into

49

the lock chamber. They vary in depth and are of uniform brightness.

"If the Ship was assembled in space the markings could have been made at any time during its construction and still appear fresh and bright. There are an awful lot of them, all over the place . . ."

"We would like a more detailed description of mechanisms in the area, if you can see any. I can't see very much with this telescope . . ."

The voice coming from P-One sounded strained, with the subtle difference in tone which labeled it for public rather than private consumption. On Earth everyone who could get within earshot of a radio or a simulated mockup on TV, would be hanging on every word—a world record for any single program. Morrison could not help being conscious of those billions of ears. Even Walters seemed to be more frightened by them than what lay inside the Ship.

The pilot took a deep and audible breath, then continued, "Six inches from the rim of the personnel lock, on the side facing aft, there is a lever about two feet long. It is set flush with the skin except at one end where a hemispherical dimple about three inches deep gives access to the handle . . ."

He was using the term loosely, McCullough thought as he photographed it, because the handle was not meant for hands. It terminated in a small knob containing two small, conical depressions on opposite sides, and it was the perfect shape for a finger and thumb, or pincers . . .

"I'm pulling it from the recess now," Walters said quickly, giving the colonel no time to have second thoughts. "I am doing it very slowly. There was resistance at first, suggesting spring loading, but now it is moving easily. This must mean a powered actuator rather than a direct linkage to the door itself. So far nothing has happened. The lever is now approximately thirty degrees along its angle of travel, approaching forty-five ... Oops!"

A brief, silent hurricane rushed out of the suddenly open airlock, and they were in the center of a globe of fog which dispersed almost as soon as it had formed. McCullough reached forward, gripped the lever and returned it to its recess. Obediently the lock swung closed. He waited a few seconds, then opened and closed it again several times.

"What is happening out there, dammit?" said the colonel furiously, momentarily forgetting the networks and their views on the sort of language suitable for family audiences. *"What are you two playing at?"*

Walters looked at McCullough before replying, then he said, "This was an idea we discussed during the trip out. Very simply, it involves us leaning over backward in doing all the right things—at least, we *hope* they are the right things. Here we are assuming that the reactions and motivations of the aliens are similar to our own where defence mechanisms and self-preservation are concerned.

"In the present situation," he went on, "we are entering their ship surreptitiously. It might even be argued that we are breaking and entering or effecting an illegal entry in that we haven't been invited to come in. The flares and radio signals during our approach may not have been noticed—they were not watching or listening, or maybe they are very alien and do not have eyes or ears. But the opening and closing of the airlock should register in a fashion understandable to them somewhere in their control center.

"What we mean is, a burglar doesn't open and close a door, or even a window, several times before entering . . ."

"Very well, I take the point. But if a stranger slammed my front door several times to let me know he was there, I might feel, well, irritated . . ."

While they were talking, McCullough investigated the open lock, shining his torch around the rim so as to show any possible observer that it was simply a source of light and not a weapon, before directing the beam into the lock chamber. It was unlikely that anyone would be waiting for them inside the lock, their situation might be more analagous to the coal cellar manhole than the front door, but McCullough wanted to establish habits of viewing each simple, innocent act as it might appear to nonhuman eyes and mentalities.

He gripped the rim of the seal with one hand and carefully moved his head and shoulders into the opening. Even though there was no interior lighting, his torch gave him a good view of the lock chamber except where the inward-opening seal blocked his vision on one side.

The basic color scheme was pale gray or pale blue-gray. Walls, ceiling and floor—it was impossible to tell which was which—were covered with disciplined masses of plumbing, grapples and what looked like lashing points for heavy stores, all color coded in vivid greens, blues and reds. The lock chamber was large, about thirty feet wide and ten deep. Set into each wall were seals four or five times the area of the one McCullough was using, and in the center of each there was a small transparent panel. He knew they were transparent because his flash showed tantalizing glimpses of other brightly painted shapes on the other side. From what he could see, this area of the Ship was in darkness.

McCullough could imagine the chamber as a transfer point for containers of food and equipment, lashed down to render them immobile until they were distributed about the Ship. Heavy equipment drifting loose in the weightless condition could be a menace to alien life and limb as well as human. But the disposition of lashing points and their support brackets suggested a lack of gravitational influence, whether natural, artificial or due to acceleration, being allowed for in the design. Which might mean that the interior of the Ship remained permanently in the weightless condition even during periods of powered flight.

Something more advanced than rocket propulsion was used on *this* Ship. But it all looked so—so unsophisticated . . .

McCullough became aware of a hand gripping his ankle and drawing him slowly out of the lock entrance, and Walters saying, "What's the matter, didn't you hear what I said?"

"When my helmet antenna was inside," said McCullough, "your voice faded to nothing. Some sort of screening effect, I suppose."

"Yes. And that is the next step, the colonel says. Checking communications between the lock interior and the P-ships."

A few minutes later the pilot entered the lock chamber and closed the seal behind him. From inside he could not make himself heard or receive the colonel's signal until he brought his antenna into contact with the metal of the hull, when two-way communication was possible although with a greatly diminished signal strength.

Walter reopened the seal and when McCullough joined him inside he closed it again.

Morrison did not sound happy over what they were doing. At the risk of disappointing the countless millions of eager listeners at home, he stated several times that his men needed rest—the next stage of the investigation was crucial and he wanted them to be fully alert. It had been almost thirty-two hours since any of them had had a proper rest period. He suspected that the two men on the Ship were becoming too tired even to talk . . .

"Sarcastic so-and-so," said Walters, momentarily breaking antenna contact with the nearby bulkhead. A tremendous, eye-watering, jaw-wrenching yawn put a great dark hole in his face and he went on, "I wasn't even tired until he reminded me! But you had better talk to him. I want to trace this cable loom running along the inside face of the chamber. The wiring seems too fine to carry much juice so it may be part of the internal communications or lighting system.

"Tell the colonel what I'm doing, along with anything else which occurs to you . . ."

McCullough did so, beginning with a minutely detailed description of the chamber and the view through its five internal windows and going on to make the first, tentative conclusions regarding the Ship and its builders.

The cable looms, conduits and plumbing were color coded in a garish variety of shades, some of them bearing permutations of other colored spots, bands or stripes. A human electronics engineer would have felt almost at home here, McCullough thought.

Fore, aft and on the floor and ceiling the chamber's transparent panels, so far as it was possible to see with a flashlight, showed a similar arrangement in the adjacent compartments. Apparently the chamber was set between the ship's outer and inner hull, in the space which contained the vessel's power, control and sensory equipment. The lock chamber, which must be one of many, would give access to the inter-hull space for purposes of repair or maintenance. The inboard-facing window gave a view which contained least of all to see—merely a section of corridor, eight feet square and of unknown length, whose four sides were covered with large-mesh netting pulled taut.

The visible mechanical and structural features gave an overall impression of crudeness. There was no sign of lightening holes or cut-outs in any of the support brackets or structural members, no indication that considerations of weight or power-mass ratios had entered into the designers' calculations . . .

". . . It is too soon to make any hard and fast assumptions about them," McCullough went on. "We *know* that they do not have fingers, and may have a two-digit pincer arrangement. Probably their visual range and sensitivity is similar to ours, judging by the color intensities used on cable identification. The, to us, crude and unnecessarily robust construction of minor structural details indicates a lack of concern over weight and the power required to get it moving. The corridor netting suggests that they are not advanced enough to possess an artificial gravity system, and the total absence of light and movement shows that the Ship is orbiting in a power-down condition . . . *Walters!*"

In the corridor outside the chamber, the lights had come on.

"Sorry, that was me," said Walters sheepishly. "I've discovered what a light switch looks like—but I must have guessed wrong." The light in the corridor went off and on several times, then suddenly the lock chamber lighting came on. He added, "Better tell the colonel about this, too."

McCullough informed the colonel that Walters had found the light switches, had experimented with them and that the Ship's illumination was a bright, bluish-white emanating from tubes which they had mistaken for sections of plumbing. There was still no reaction from the alien crew, and McCullough was beginning to wonder if the Ship had a crew . . .

"You two seem to have a weakness for slamming doors and switching lights on! However, this wraps it up for the time being. We need rest. Return to P-Two—we have a lot to think about before we do anything else on that ship. Say so if you understand."

"Understood, sir," said Walters. "But we would like a sample of Ship's air before we leave. Five minutes should do it."

McCullough was beginning to feel irritable and very tired and he did want the chance to analyze as soon as possible whatever atmosphere it was that the aliens breathed. But the thought kept recurring to him that he was not being very cautious about this, that he was breaking even his own rules, and that fatigue was a little like drunkenness in that it made people take chances.

Walters opened the corridor seal and the alien air roared into the lock chamber. Their suits lost their taut, puffy appearance and hung loosely against their bodies. Ship pressure seemed to be a pound or two per square inch higher than suit pressure, McCullough thought as he took the sample. The pilot was moving toward the open seal.

"I'm only going to take a look," said Walters.

McCullough joined him.

There was only one source of light in the corridor, the one switched on by Walters, so that both ends disappeared into blackness. But suddenly McCullough felt the wall netting vibrate and—*something*— was shooting toward them along the corridor . . .

McCullough flung himself back, but Walters, who had a leg and arm outside the rim at the time, fumbled and was slower getting in. The doctor had a glimpse of something rushing past the opening, something which looked a little like a heavy, leathery starfish, then Walters reached the lock actuator and the seal slammed closed.

The pilot remained floating with one hand gripping the actuator lever and the other resting ludicrously on his hip. His face was white and sweating and his eyes were squeezed shut.

"It can't get in, now—we're safe—" began McCullough, then stopped.

Walters was not safe. There was a large, triangular tear in the fabric of his suit at the right hip. The undergarment showed through it, also a section of the air-conditioning system looking strangely like a bared artery, although the leg itself did not appear to be injured.

The pilot was trying to hold the tear closed with his hand. But it was too big, the edges were too ragged and the pressure difference was too great to keep the alien atmosphere from forcing its way into his suit.

He began to cough.

chapter eight

MORE THAN ANYTHING else he had ever wanted in
his whole life, McCullough wanted out. Never before
had the cramped and stinking confines of the command module seemed so desirable and secure. And
P-Two was drifting less than a hundred yards away,
with Berryman on watch ready to help him inside
and take him away from this suddenly frightful
place. All he had to do was operate one childishly
simple lever.

It would mean evacuating the chamber, of course.
Walters would die of explosive decompression. But
the pilot was strangling to death in an alien atmosphere anyway and the other might be quicker and
more merciful . . .

Except that Berryman might not want to leave
without Walters, and explosive decompression was
not a nice way to die, and in his student days
McCullough had been pretty thoroughly conditioned
against mercy killing . . .

"Doctor," said Walters between coughs, "do you have—a band-aid on you?"

"What?" said McCullough, then added with feeling, "Dammit, I'm *stupid!*"

A length of adhesive with its washable plastic backing would not hold the tear together in vacuo, but with pressure almost equal between chamber and suit interior it would act as a barrier to the entry of the alien air all around them—for a time, at least. Quickly McCullough took a dressing from his kit and pressed the edges of the tear together while Walters rubbed on the tape.

When they were finished McCullough said, "How do you feel? Any pain in the chest? Nausea? Impairment of vision . . . ?"

Walters shook his head. Almost strangling himself with his effort not to cough, he said, "The—the smell is like ammonia—or formaldehyde. Strong and sharp but not—a stinking smell. But you'd better tell the colonel."

McCullough nodded and laid his antenna against the metal wall.

The colonel interrupted him only once to ask what the pilot had been doing out in the corridor, then he told McCullough to continue with his report without trying to make excuses for Walters' stupidity. The doctor did so, spending less time on the incident itself than on the problems it had raised.

"Can you tie off the leg section tightly enough to avoid a lethal pressure drop for the few minutes it will take to get him back to P-Two? It would mean decompressing the leg, of course, but that would be better than . . ."

"No, sir. The tear is high on the left hip. We can't evacuate the chamber while he is in it, and I can't leave and nobody from outside can enter unless . . ."

". . . *Unless Walters goes back into the corridor while the chamber is airless. Ask him how he feels about doing that.*"

The pilot's reply had to be edited and censored considerably. McCullough said, "He'll do it, but he doesn't feel too enthusiastic."

Morrison refused to comment on Walters' feelings. He said, "*That takes care of your return, but getting him back to P-Two means putting him in another suit . . .*"

There were several good reasons why the P-ships did not carry spare spacesuits. Quite apart from the extra weight and stowage requirements involved, there was the fact that a spacesuit had to be literally tailored to fit its wearer, and this would have meant carrying a spare for every member of the expedition. As well, damage to a suit usually meant death for its wearer, so that repairs were not even considered. In any case, repairing a suit was a specialist's job requiring facilities not available on the ships.

"*Both Hollis and Berryman are close to Walters in size,*" the colonel went on, "*and Berryman is closest in distance. I'll shoot Drew across to you. While he's on the way, Berryman can place his suit in P-Two's airlock. Drew will pick it up and deliver it to you for Walters and collect your air sample.*

"*You, Doctor, will stay with Walters to see that his seals are tight and the suit isn't strained dangerously by forcing the fit. As well as losing one of our trained pilots, we can't afford to write off another suit. What is his condition now?*"

Walters had his antenna in contact with the plating, listening. He tried to speak, broke into a fit of coughing, and made a rude gesture instead.

McCullough translated, "He has a persistent cough which may be due to throat irritation only. There are no other respiratory symptoms, no chest pain and no detectable toxic affects. His morale is good." The doctor did not *know* these things with any degree of certainty—his optimism was mostly for his patient's benefit. But just in case the colonel did not realize what McCullough was doing, he added quickly, "But I'd like to give him a thorough check-up in shirt-sleeve conditions as soon as possible."

A little later Morrison told them Drew was on his way and that he was moving his own ship in to join P-Two. Tactically this was not a good move, he said, but on this occasion tactics and common sense seemed to be at variance, and in any case they could pull out quickly if it became necessary.

"And go home?" asked McCullough.

"I don't know, Doctor. There are other considerations."

As the period of high drama, the first and unfortunately violent contact with the aliens passed, the colonel began to worry over the possibility that Prometheus Control had not faded out the networks during the incident with Walters and the alien. Aware suddenly of a possible audience, they became laconic to the point of sounding ridiculous. Stiffly, the colonel wished Walters good luck. Walters said, "Thanks." Berryman suggested McCullough should make a sketch of the alien from memory while they were waiting on Drew. Morrison said it was a good idea, just in case. Nobody asked in case of what.

During the twenty minutes or so it took for Drew to reach them—in subjective time it felt more like ten years—McCullough sketched the alien and made a map of the vicinity of their lock chamber. While doing so he discovered a leak in one of the pipe joints. Probably the repeated opening and closing of the seal had put an unfair strain on the hydraulic system—the joint was sweating and droplets of a clear brownish liquid hung around it, steaming faintly.

McCullough hoped nothing calamitous would happen when the chamber was evacuated.

Drew arrived, checked by radio on the operation of the lock, then waited while McCullough opened the inner seal and entered the corridor with Walters. As the air rushed out of the chamber and Drew swam in, a fogginess appeared around the leaking joint, but nothing else seemed to be happening.

There were no aliens visible in the lighted section of corridor.

"If one of them comes at us," McCullough told Walters, "I'll hang onto the net and kick at it with both feet. You concentrate on holding that patch in position."

He was beginning to feel that the pilot's trouble had been his own rather than Walters' fault.

The leak in the lock's hydraulic system was bothering him. It was almost certainly a recent malfunction. There was a strong probability that it had occurred because the seal actuator mechanism had been recently overstressed. McCullough had forgotten how many times exactly they had opened and closed the thing, something like seventeen or eighteen times in as many minutes, while the chances were that normal usage was in the order of twice a day.

He was assuming, of course, that these were not omnipotent aliens and that their ship might occasionally develop mechanical faults. Such failures would show in their control center and a member of the crew might be sent to check on it, or perhaps to deal with the real cause of the trouble—the human invaders. McCullough was coming to realize that their actions, which had been meant simply to advertise their presence on board, could just as well be construed as criminally irresponsible or wantonly destructive. In these circumstances a certain amount of hostility on the part of the aliens would be understandable.

People who leaned over backward, McCullough thought grimly, frequently fell flat on their face . . .

"Walters. Doctor." Drew's voice came suddenly. "The colonel sent you a weapon of sorts. To be used only in self-defense, he says. Grip it in the middle and stab with it like a spear."

McCullough looked up and down the still empty corridor, then into the chamber. He said, "It's just a length of pipe."

"A blunt bayonet makes a worse mess than a sharp one," Drew said cheerfully, "and a length of one-inch pipe is about as blunt as a weapon can get. Just take time to aim and jab hard—I guarantee it will discourage any man or beastie not wearing a suit of armor. I'm leaving now. Good luck . . ."

A few seconds later he was blown through the outer door by escaping air, and another eternity passed while he jetted back to the hull and closed it again. Walters and McCullough re-entered the chamber, still without alien interference.

The problem now was to get Walters out of his damaged suit and into the replacement quickly enough to keep him from being gassed. McCullough started by opening the pilot's face-plate, taping up his nostrils and making him breathe slowly through his oxygen line. Then he wrapped his legs around the pilot's waist and began cutting away the damaged suit.

It was hard, painstaking work. The plastic and metal foil was difficult to cut with a scalpel and McCullough was all too aware of the skin and blood vessels lying just a fraction of an inch below. The drying unit in his own suit refused to cope with the increased flow of perspiration, his visor was fogging badly despite its special coating, and he wasn't dissipating nearly enough of his body heat.

This would be a great time to pass out from heat stroke.

Quickly he slit the legs, arms and chest, peeling them away to leave only the shoulder section which contained the air supply and hinged-back helmet. There followed a weightless adagio dance and he drew the new suit onto the pilot's legs and arms while the tatters of the old one hung out from his back. Walters could not give him much help because the alien atmosphere was making his eyes stream and no matter how hard he tried he could not stop coughing—which drew more of the stuff into his lungs. By the time he told Walters to hyperventilate and hold his breath while the changeover was completed, McCullough was afraid that he had already breathed in too much of it.

Finally they were ready to leave. The discarded suit twisted slowly, like some shredded, dismembered corpse, in the mist which was growing visibly in the area of the leak. McCullough wondered what the aliens would make of it, what they would infer and deduce regarding the human race. The thought made him look toward the transparent panel in the door.

There were three of them.

McCullough pushed himself toward the corridor door without thinking—the reason for doing it seemed to come after the action rather than before. To Walters he said quickly, "If they open that door the outer one won't open—there's sure to be a safety interlock system—and if they see us trying to leave they will surely open it. I'll move close to the window and block their view while you open the outer seal—the suction will pull us out. Where's that blasted pipe?"

He couldn't see it. Probably it was hiding in plain sight against a background of Ship plumbing, a tree hiding in a forest.

His idea was to hold their attention somehow while blocking their view of what Walters was doing. To do so he had to get close to the transparent door panel and either arouse their interest or frighten them away. McCullough did not know of anything he could do which would prove fascinating to the aliens, but he just might be able to worry them a little with his camera.

It was a beautiful instrument which fairly bristled with supplementary lenses and attachments. It might very easily be mistaken for a weapon.

In some deep recess of his mind a small voice was reminding him insistently of the need to consider the alien point of view, and to do nothing to give them the wrong idea about humanity and human behavior. McCullough felt a moment's shame, but he was really much too frightened to listen.

There was no perceptible reaction from the e-t's as McCullough drifted up to the window, still aiming his camera. One of them was drifting in the center of the corridor, a stubby, dumbbell shape covered with long spikes. Each half of its body was roughly the size of a football, and there were no sensory or manipulatory organs visible. A second alien clung to the opposite wall net like a great, fleshy spider, giving him a perfect view of the starfish body with its thick tentacles and leathery tegument. The tentacles ended in bony pincers, like white, miniature elephant tusks. McCullough estimated its physical mass to be approximately half that of a man, with the tentacle length between four and five feet.

The third alien was of the same species as number Two. It covered part of the window with its body so that McCullough and his camera had a perfect view of its underbelly, which was soft and pinkish-brown and convoluted into folds and openings which were evidently mouths or gills or sensory equipment of some kind, all grouped around a large, sharp, centrally placed horn or sting . . .

McCullough swallowed hard. He thought that on the purely physical evidence these were not nice people.

Then suddenly the aliens began to move. McCullough still wasn't sure where their eyes were, but somehow he knew that their focus of attention had changed. Something was approaching along the corridor. He could not get his eyes close enough to the window to see, although he could hear low, gobbling sounds being transmitted through the metal of the door to his helmet. Quickly he stopped down his lens and aimed it along the dark corridor. It had a wider angle of view and might see more than he could.

The first three aliens were leaving.

Walters opened the outer seal at that moment and the rush of escaping air drew him away from the door, spinning him slowly end over end. But not before he had a glimpse of something covered with white fur, or perhaps clothing, which flicked past the window.

chapter nine

"I FEEL AN awful fool," said McCullough, looking apologetically at Walters. "I should have realized it in the Ship. At very least I should have suspected it when I examined him here . . ."

"Granted that changing suits in the corridor would have been easier on Walters' throat and eyes, I doubt if you would have been allowed to complete the operation when the aliens arrived. So you have nothing to reproach yourself with, and those photographs you took—well, altogether it was a very nice job."

"And *I'm* not complaining," said Walters.

For the analysis of the air sample taken in the corridor had shown that the alien atmosphere was not harmful to human beings and was, in fact, much less toxic than the air of an average city. But the sample taken in the lock chamber contained a quantity of vaporized liquid which could only have come from the leak in the hydraulic system. Apparently the stuff Walters had breathed was about as damaging as a similar quantity of tear gas.

But McCullough had conducted his examination of the hapless pilot as if he had been engaged on a slightly premature post-mortem . . .

"Now we must decide what to do next. I'd like the doctor and major Walters to put forward any suggestions they may have. After all, you two have more Ship experience than anyone else. How do you see the situation now?"

"I can't see anything," Walters said hoarsely. "My throat is too sore . . ."

There was an irritated, overamplified sigh from the speaker grill. McCullough nodded quickly to Walters, thought for a moment, then began to speak.

So far as he was concerned, the trip inside the alien vessel had not answered any of the major questions regarding its origin and purpose. It remained a hulking brute of a ship nearly half a mile long, orbiting the sun at a distance of one hundred and sixty million miles, seemingly in a powered-down condition and refusing to acknowledge all signals. The precision with which it had been inserted into orbit, together with the reactions of what must have been a damage-control party of its crew, seemed to rule out the earlier theory that the Ship was in a derelict or distressed condition.

Present indications were that it was deliberately refusing contact because it was here merely to conduct a survey of some description. Perhaps they did not want contact with an inferior race, or had orders forbidding such contact. McCullough was very careful to use the word 'survey' rather than 'reconnaissance,' but he was afraid the people at home would jump to conclusions no matter which word he used.

So far as the physical structure of the Ship was concerned, photographic and other observations made it clear that it had not been designed to withstand massive accelerations or even a takeoff from an average planet. However, if the netting they had observed covered all the corridors in the ship, it was unlikely that they had gravity control either inside the ship or as a means of propulsion. Since there were no rocket ventris or any other visible signs of conventional reaction propulsion capable of moving such a massive vessel, it seemed obvious that whatever method of propulsion was being used, the ship remained in the weightless condition whether it was under power or not.

Where the crew of the alien ship was concerned, they had a little more to go on.

"In addition to the physiological details in the photographs," McCullough went on, "which will tell us a lot when we have a chance to study them properly, we know that the crew is composed of three distinct species. The alien with the white fur or clothing seemed to be in a position of authority or influence over the others—even though their curiosity regarding us must have been intense, they left the area as soon as Type Three appeared."

McCullough went on, "The second type, which we encountered first when Walters was attacked, is much more aggressive or impulsive than Type Three. As I see it, the Three is their equivalent of an officer, while the Twos are a damage-control party of crew members who were angered by the damage to their lock's hydraulic system, and expressed their anger by taking a swipe at Walters. But if we assume that their orders were to ignore us and let the repairs wait until after we had gone away, and Type Three arrived on the scene to remind the others of their orders in no uncertain terms and to chase them off ..."

"They followed the Three," Walters put in. "It didn't chase them ..."

"I don't think that matters," said McCullough, then continued, "Taking a swipe at one of us is, in the circumstances, an understandable reaction. It is not a friendly reaction, of course, but it does show that we have certain emotional responses in common which could form a basis for a wider understanding in time—*if* we are allowed to maintain contact with them.

"I, personally, do not think we will be.

"For there can be no doubt that they know we are here," McCullough ended seriously. "Perhaps they have known about us from the moment we left Earth. But we are not welcome here and we should leave before they take more positive steps to discourage us."

For a long time there was silence, then Berryman said, "Surely we've come too far just to turn and run. We can investigate and photograph those hyperdrive blisters, or whatever they are, without actually entering the Ship. I agree it is good sense to run away, but make it tomorrow or sometime next week ..."

"*I—I agree,*" said Hollis from P-One. The overamplification which made the colonel's voice sound authoritative simply magnified the physicist's timidity. "*Accurate photographs of those generators —which must be connected with their propulsion system—might not give us everything we want to know, but they would at least keep our people from following too many useless avenues of research.*

"At the same time I agree with the doctor. We should not go into the Ship again if we aren't welcome . . ."

There came a sound of Morrison's throat being cleared, and Hollis broke off. Obviously the colonel was willing for the other to speak so long as he said the right things, and talking about leaving was not one of the right things, so it was equally obvious that the colonel also wanted to stay.

Walters found his voice suddenly and said, "We made a mistake by damaging their lock mechanism, but that doesn't necessarily mean they will chase us away like small boys caught robbing an orchard! That would be too—too petty an act for a race capable of interstellar flight . . ."

"I'd like to think so, too," McCullough said sharply. "But I keep remembering the petty things we did in the sailing ship and stagecoach era, and how many of us are still doing them."

"But we're unarmed!" Berryman broke in. "Our ships are downright primitive by their standards. And in a sense we belong to the same club. Space travel is not as dangerous for them as for us, of course, but . . ."

"But you feel," McCullough finished for him, with a sarcastic edge to his voice, "that the alien captain should pipe the plucky primitives aboard with full honors. Don't you think it possible that this sort of thing may have happened many times to this particular ship? Maybe they are a little tired of primitives busting a gut to get out to look over their ships. So much so, perhaps, that they won't even toss a metaphorical coin into the water to see us do tricks for them because of the danger of us fouling their metaphorical propellors."

"Walters' idea of the alien might be too noble," Berryman protested, "but your's is too base and cynical. This isn't like you, Doctor."

"No indeed," said Walters, stifling a cough. "And aren't we forgetting that practically *all* of this is sheer guesswork? They might not be noble or base. They might not even be all that far advanced technically, judging by their ship's construction. And I don't think we should run away until we at least know what we are running away from. McCullough is completely off-base in this."

"Calm down, gentlemen. We are not going to leave, not immediately and not even next week. It seems Control have been keeping us in the dark—for our peace of mind, they say—about certain new developments which makes it necessary for us to stay put. The period mentioned was a minimum of three weeks.

"You see, our people were a little late in cutting the transmission to the networks when things became exciting at the Ship, and the political side effects have yet to be evaluated. At the present time I am receiving new, modified, amended or downright contradictory orders on an average of three times a day . . ."

The incident on the Ship had gone out in its entirety, via translators or commentators where non-English speaking nations were concerned, to practically everyone on Earth. Prometheus had wanted to cut transmission, but a quite incredible amount of pressure had been brought to bear on them to continue relaying the signals from the Alien—it was already being capitalized and used in the same sentences with words like Invader and Enemy—so far as the colonel knew, they would still receive everything he sent. He had used his discretion, however, regarding the signals recently received from P-Two.

Already there was talk of trebling NASA's appropriation, building an armada, knitting warm sweaters —public reaction was fluid and still somewhat confused, but the general feeling was that something positive should be done. It was being suggested that the U.S. and Russia pool their space capability against the common enemy . . .

". . . The Russians would already be out here with us if they hadn't jumped the gun by launching that rather ambitious manned Venus Orbiting Station just before the Ship appeared, and their present capability may be stretched to the limit keeping it supplied. However, if our stay out here becomes extended, Biakonur have offered Prometheus the use of two of their high-acceleration supply vehicles, with no strings attached other than that they must not be used to carry weapons.

"You will appreciate the political implications which have grown out of our handling of this situation—our bungled handling of the first contact, some say. The U.N. are being quite critical . . .

"But now we must try to devise tactics to cover this situation. You are all free to interrupt and offer suggestions at any time . . ."

The first interruption came within seconds, from Berryman, who suggested very strongly that it would be a criminal waste of opportunity to run away without trying to find out a little more about alien science and, if possible, culture, adding that any tactics used against the aliens must be purely defensive. Hollis, Walters and McCullough interrupted to agree with this, and Drew said that considering the relative sizes of the vessels concerned, they had no choice.

Irritated, Morrison replied that he had no intention of declaring war on anybody, and would they all please make their suggestions more constructive and less general in nature.

Finally it was decided that P-One and P-Two would be joined together nose-to-nose. There was provision for doing this in design, and the result would be that Walters would have access to both command modules without having to don a spacesuit. There would also be a saving in power by having one life-support system serve two ships, since it might come about that the other men would be absent on the alien Ship for extended periods of time. The duties of this single watch-keeping officer would be to maintain contact with the men investigating the alien vessel and Prometheus Control, and to report progress.

Drew had a lot to say on the subject of defensive weapons. They had no intention of hurting, much less killing, anyone on the alien Ship. But if they did re-enter the vessel, they would have to have a means of protecting themselves and their irreplaceable spacesuits from injury. With the aid of the doctor's as yet incomplete physiological data on the known alien life-forms, they devised and built a prototype weapon, rather like a ski stick, which would fend off aliens and prick them lightly if they became too persistent.

They discussed alien motivation and possible methods of communication at great length, and somehow it became an accepted, although not formally agreed fact that they *would* go aboard the alien Ship again . . .

Many hours later, while they were closing with P-One for the docking operation, Walters said hoarsely, "I'm sorry for what I said back there, Doctor. But you put up such a good, sensible case for leaving, I thought the colonel might decide there and then to do just that, and this is such a unique opportunity for—for . . ."

"Getting clobbered?" Berryman asked, grinning. He went on, "But I wouldn't apologize, Walters, if I were you. It seems to me that if your mind was capable of really devious thinking, and if you weren't just an *amateur* psychologist, you would have realized by now that he was indulging in a piece of psychological sleight of hand. Probably he had it all worked out with the colonel in advance— talking good, sound common sense, verbalizing all our own secret fears and survival instincts, then making us argue against them to show how superior we thought we were to him. In short, and to mix a metaphor slightly, propping up our weakening resolve with an obviously broken reed.

"Not that he is likely to admit any of this, of course."

They were both staring at him.

McCullough felt his face burning, but deep inside him there was another and much more pleasant feeling of warmth. It occurred to him suddenly that there were none so blind as those who could see perfectly, but shut their eyes because they happened to be looking at a friend.

"It's a thought," said McCullough. To himself he added, *A happy afterthought . . .*

chapter ten

As THE ONLY member of the expedition with both a spacesuit and firsthand alien experience, McCullough was placed in charge of the second boarding party. Those were the reasons given by Morrison and, without actually saying so, the others gave McCullough the impression that they considered it a sensible arrangement.

Five minutes after leaving the P-ships, however, Morrison was no longer even pretending that McCullough was in charge.

The entry point chosen was a personnel lock about one hundred yards aft of the first one. McCullough operated the seal mechanism and entered, followed by the colonel, Berryman, Hollis and Drew. This time he did not slam the door or test the hydraulic actuator to destruction. Inside he demonstrated the working of the light switches. The chamber differed only in detail from the previous one, but this time they were going to examine the fine details.

There were no aliens in the lock chamber or in the corridor outside.

Morrison had brought a spotlight from P-One. Using the access doors on four sides of the chamber and the large transparent panels set into them, he mapped the space between the Ship's double hull while Drew kept watch on the corridor and reported progress to Walters on P-Two. Berryman, Hollis and McCullough scoured the place for identification numbers.

"I realize," said Berryman during the first few minutes of the examination, "that robust construction together with simplicity of design is supposed to reduce the danger of component failure, but this angle bracket is so simple it is downright crude!"

But the badly finished support bracket, like all the other small structural members they were examining, possessed the expected symbols of identification.

Their idea was simply that any piece of machinery beyond a certain degree of complexity—from a car or light aeroplane up to and including spaceships half a mile long—required an enormous amount of prior design work, planning and tooling long before the first simple parts and subassemblies became three-dimensional metal on someone's workbench. The number of general assembly and detail drawings, material specification charts, wiring diagrams and so on for a vessel of this size must have been mind-staggering, and the purpose of all this paperwork was simply to instruct people of *average intelligence* in the manufacture and fitting together of the parts in this gigantic three-dimensional jigsaw puzzle.

If normal human practice was observed—and the aircraft engineers who had lectured them on the trip out insisted that there was no easier way short of waving a magic wand—then these drawings together with the components they described must include exact instructions for the placing of these parts within the jigsaw.

It was possible that the aliens had some exotic method of identifying components—such as impressing each part with a telepathic identity tag, or tactile coding systems instead of using visible printed symbols. But considering the size of the project and the tremendous number of parts to be identified, they were fairly sure that the aliens would do it the easy way, which was to mark the surface material of the component with symbols which could be read at a glance.

The system used on the Ship seemed to be some kind of vibro-etch technique. It was nice to know that, in the philosophy of aircraft and spaceship construction at least, the e-t's and humans thought alike.

"You notice there are no curved lines in these symbols," said Hollis at one point. "The result of having pincers instead of fingers and an opposable thumb, would you say, Doctor?"

"Not necessarily," said McCullough. "If we had continued to use Roman instead of Arabic numerals . . ."

"Discuss your findings later, gentlemen," said Morrison impatiently. "We will take a quick look along the corridor. Berryman and I will move aft, Hollis and McCullough forward, and Drew will guard the lock chamber. Go only as far as the first intersection—that should make it impossible for any of us to be cut off. Make a map showing door positions and anything else of interest. If the doors have transparent panels, shoot whatever you can get a picture of and sketch in room dimensions and contents of what you can't shoot.

"Be as quick as you can," he ended. "If you meet anything, retreat or defend yourselves without hurting it. All right, Drew, crack the seal."

They split up as directed, McCullough keeping slightly ahead of Hollis so as not to prod him with his ridiculous weapon. Since the Ship seemed to be designed for free fall conditions there was no clearly defined floor, ceiling or walls in the corridor. The netting was supported a few inches out from each wall and stretched taut and was interrupted at regular intervals by the entrances to what seemed to be storerooms. Being cautious men, they shone their lights only into the rooms whose doors had transparent panels in them and left the others alone even though they would have opened at a touch—they were simple, sliding doors rather than pressure seals. Every door bore two sets of identifying symbols placed upside down to each other so as to be easily read whatever the direction of approach.

Lighting fixtures and switches were set at intervals along the corridor, but McCullough did not turn them on. The torches of Hollis and himself gave enough light at short range and there was no point in letting the aliens in their control room know that the humans had moved into the corridor.

At the intersection, one corridor continued forward while another curved away in each direction, following the lateral curvature of the hull so that they could see only twenty yards or so along it. Just at the limit of vision in each branch there were the mouths of two other corridors paralleling their own.

"If we went back along one of them," said Hollis,

pointing, "and then took the first outboard turning, we should meet up with the colonel and Berryman."

"Do you want to try it?" said McCullough.

"No," said Hollis.

The physicist busied himself with his sketch pad while McCullough kept watch in four directions. But they were not disturbed by anything until the colonel's voice ordered them back to the lock chamber.

Ten minutes later they were outside the Ship again and heading for a lock close to one of the big transparent blisters. Hollis was literally babbling with excitement over the prospect of tinkering with a real live—Walters on P-Two warned that it was probably several million volts live—hyperspatial generator. McCullough said nothing and thought seriously about Colonel Morrison's voice.

Morrison had the irritating habit of using too much volume during transmission and sounding like a short-tempered hurler of thunderbolts rather than the simple voice of authority. But now the doctor was beginning to wonder if the overamplification and, perhaps, the judicious use of the tone control to make it sound deeper as well as louder, was the sole reason for Morrison's stern-sounding, authoritative tone. Certainly the difference in his natural and radio voice was amazing. McCullough had the uncomfortable feeling that every time the colonel opened his mouth in ordinary face-to-face conversation he nibbled away a little of his own authority.

It was becoming obvious that the Colonel Morrison whom Berryman, Walters and he himself knew as a voice from P-One was not necessarily the same person Drew and Hollis knew on the colonel's own ship. It was becoming much easier to believe Morrison capable of gossiping like an old woman to

Drew while excluding Hollis and allowing the physicist to get into the sorry state McCullough had found him in when he had been shot across to the other ship.

At the same time McCullough knew that he must guard against a too sudden reversal of feeling. One unexpected weakness—especially in an area so susceptible to misinterpretation as a tone of voice—did not mean that the colonel was automatically weak, ineffectual and unsuited to wield authority and had, therefore, no right to their obedience.

McCullough worried about the colonel all the way to their next point of entry.

This time they stayed only a few minutes in the lock chamber and did not go into the corridor at all. Access to the space between outer and inner hulls was by a simple, unpressurized sliding door, and the air on the other side of it was at corridor pressure. Masses of cable conduits, plumbing and enigmatic cabinets sprouted among a forest of girders on all sides, except where a narrow ladder of netting stretched forward through a tunnel cleared in the metallic jungle. At the other end of the ladder the colonel's spotlight showed the entrance, if their calculations were correct, to one of the blisters.

"Use our own lighting," Morrison said, "and don't wander away from the net. We might accidentally short-circuit something and kill ourselves."

"I don't think so, sir," said Berryman. "The cables all seem to be well insulated."

"I agree," said Hollis, "but we should examine the markings on cables entering the blister to help us separate lighting and instrumentation circuits from power lines."

"Be careful anyway!" said the colonel sharply.

"Drew, guard the lock chamber. The rest of you follow me."

Two days ago Berryman might have argued against the colonel like that, McCullough thought, but not Hollis.

The atmosphere remained tense until they entered the blister through an airlock. Inside they found no atmosphere at all. This did not surprise Hollis who said that he had expected the generators to operate in a vacuum. A few minutes later they discovered that the vacuum was maintained by having the blister open to space, although the openings in the transparent canopy were too narrow to allow passage to a man or, McCullough suspected, an alien. Sunlight flooded through the transparent plastic, throwing dazzling highlights off the bare metal and pale blue ceramics all around them. The two P-ships were clearly visible in the black sky and the canopy was no barrier to communications.

"There are bare power lines in this room," said the colonel stiffly, "so be careful."

"Yes, sir," said Hollis quickly. "But I don't think there will be any danger from them—the generator isn't switched on. At the same time, it will take weeks to study this place properly and I should like to make absolutely sure of our safety while doing so."

His idea was to short the power lines where they entered the blister. He was fairly sure that the generator's design incorporated protective fusing and similar fail-safe devices so that the valuable generator itself would not be destroyed. If *he* was building the thing, that was how Hollis would do it. There was perhaps no need for him to point out that this intricate piece of equipment was *not* a crudely built structure—it looked as if it had been put together by watchmakers.

It was also possible that the generator would not operate if foreign bodies—themselves—were present in the blister. At the same time Hollis said he would feel much more comfortable investigating the place when he was less likely at any moment to be struck by alien lightning.

"You're the physicist," said the colonel. "But it occurs to me that spiking one of their generators will make them feel annoyed. Even more annoyed than slamming an airlock door!"

Instead of netting, a rigid plastic ladder arrangement curved around and through the masses of equipment projecting into the blister, twisting and widening out into an outsize tennis racket shape where it was obvious that more than one alien was meant to work on it. Hollis did not talk during the investigation except for the single occasion when he told McCullough with great fervor that his camera contained the most valuable pictures ever taken.

But McCullough was only half listening to him. He had the feeling that they were all being too enthusiastic, not worrying nearly enough about the people of the Ship and what they would think of all this and generally tending to forget where they were. Maybe they wanted to forget where they were, of course, and the enthusiasm and lack of proper thought were aids to accomplishing this, but McCullough had the awful feeling that they should all stop and have a good, long think.

He wished Morrison would take a firm grip on the situation and *make* them stop and think!

The colonel's last remark had brought back to his mind the name of the old-time author responsible for a story called 'First Contact.' He had also written one entitled 'The Ethical Equations' and during the trip out, they had talked over these and a great many other fictional first contacts—science fiction data being the only kind available to them—and the ethical equations had been very thoroughly discussed.

They had all gained, McCullough now realized, much comfort from them.

In substance the equations stated that if one did a person or an alien a good turn, an equal reward would ultimately be forthcoming, and that the same would apply if someone did something wrong. Eventually an exact balance of punishment or reward would occur. Assuming then that the crew of the alien Ship did, after their own fashion, subscribe to this ethic, what had the human boarding party done that was inherently, basically wrong?

They were guilty of blundering into a situation which they did not understand. They had damaged alien property and they were guilty of trespass. Their intentions had not been evil, of course, but that fact would not be apparent to the aliens. However, an intelligent extraterrestrial species capable of crossing interstellar space should possess enough understanding or empathy to credit another intelligent species with the normal amount of scientific curiosity, and the sins of trespass and minor property damage were venial to say the least.

But in the deeper recesses of his brain, in the levels of mind which operated on hunches and guesswork and insufficient data, McCullough refused to be reassured or even comforted. To the contrary, his fear mounted steadily with every hour that passed. And when Walter's voice sounded suddenly in his 'phones he started so violently that he almost lost his camera.

"Sir!" said the pilot. *"Drew reports activity in the corridor outside his position. Five Type Twos along the corridor in the direction of your blister. He had the lock chamber lights switched on and saw them clearly, though they didn't see him."*

"Everybody out!" said the colonel. "Hurry it up! We'll go back the way we came, avoiding the corridor. I—I don't think we should attempt a formal contact just yet . . ."

"He also says there is something like a Type One in the interhull space, clinging to the netting."

"We'll ignore it," said Morrison, "and hope it does the same. Hollis, *move!"*

They went through the blister lock and along the net, with Morrison leading, Hollis and McCullough facing each other on opposite sides of the netting and Berryman bringing up the rear. They pulled themselves hand over hand toward Drew and the opened lock chamber while their eyes searched the dark spaces between the cabinets and masses of plumbing on all sides of them.

"Doctor!"

Morrison's spotlight had picked out a small, bristling alien, something like a Siamese twin porcupine, which was flip-flopping along the net away from them. McCullough still could not see what it used for hands.

"Got it," he said, replacing his camera and hurrying on.

Drew had taken up a classic defensive position outside the open door, crouching with one leg hooked into the net to steady himself. The haft of his ski stick was wedged against the wall plating with the business end pointing back the way they had come. A little self-consciously, Morrison took up a similar position on the other side of the opening and waved the others through.

McCullough entered first, then Hollis. They turned to assist Berryman then, and had a hand under each armpit when it happened.

His radio went into a howl of oscillation as four voices tried to use it at the same time, and McCullough saw aliens swarming toward them out of the dark spaces between the supposedly solid masses of equipment. Morrison and Drew he could not see at all. The colonel had lost his spotlight, and Berryman was being pulled away from them.

One of the aliens had anchored itself to the combing with two of its tentacles while the other two were wrapped around the pilot's feet. Another e-t had swarmed onto his back, its sting jabbing furiously—McCullough could hear it clanking against Berryman's air tanks. He knew that it had only to shift its position by a few inches for the pilot to be very horribly dead.

chapter eleven

For several seconds McCullough could do nothing except stare in fascination at the colonel's spotlight as it was sent spinning to and fro by the struggling, colliding bodies around the entrance. Lit by that wildly rotating beam the scene took on the flickering, unreal quality of an old-time silent film. The spotlight was blinding and confusing the men as much as the aliens, because it was some time before McCullough realized that Berryman had freed one foot and was using it to kick at the tentacle holding the other—he had been viewing the operation as a series of disconnected stills.

Hollis was mouthing at him—the suit radio still emitted a constant howl of oscillation because too many people were trying to use it at the same time—and pointing at the wall net. The physicist was on his knees beside the sliding door and had worked his feet and lower legs between the net and the wall. McCullough got the idea and did the same, and together they took a firm, two-handed grip on each of Berryman's arms and pulled hard.

Berryman came free of the first alien so suddenly that his visor cracked against the edge of the opening and the force of the pull sent him shooting past so quickly that they had to grab his feet. The second alien was still clinging to his back, still stabbing at his air tanks.

A pair of legs were coming through the opening. McCullough gave one of them a tug to help whoever it was on their way. There were long tears in the fabric covering one leg and blood was oozing out of one of them.

The constant howling made it difficult to think.

They pulled Berryman down between them, hooked his legs into the netting, then concentrated their efforts on the alien clinging to his back. Its tentacles were still wrapped tightly around the pilot's chest, and Hollis pushed the butt of a ski stick between the alien's underbelly and Berryman's back and tried to lever it away. The alien jerked violently—Hollis must have prodded a sensitive area—but did not let go. Then McCullough discovered the answer. If they reached under Berryman's chest and gripped the tentacles by their tips, they could be peeled back relatively easily.

There was a muffled clang. McCullough looked round quickly and saw that everyone was inside. Drew was slotting his weapon into the piping which ran along both sides of the sliding door and through the ring handle so as to form a bar. Possibly the aliens could open it, but not without tearing out a chunk of their hydraulic system.

The howling in his earphones was beginning to break into fragments of words and sentences.

". . . My suit's torn. I'm losing air . . . Get it off me! Get it off . . . Shut up, all of you, and . . . Stop it wriggling or it will stab . . . My leg, dammit, where's the doctor? Off your radio and open your visors . . . Quiet, and open your helmets . . . !

McCullough kept quiet as ordered, realizing suddenly that he himself had been contributing as much as everyone else to the uproar. But he did not open his visors because his hands were full of alien tentacles.

For the few minutes it took to pull the twisting, heaving body off Berryman's back, McCullough had a really close look at the alien. There was a shallow recess between the roots of its tentacles, set so low as to be almost on the edge of its underbelly, and in it there was the soft, wet gleam of something which could only be an eye. The opening and closing mechanism seemed to be a double-lid arrangement operating vertically rather than horizontally and the eye was quite definitely looking at him. The ends of its tentacles quivered as they tried to pull away, and for some odd reason McCullough was reminded of the big, stupid, friendly dog he had had once and of the time he had tried to teach it to shake hands.

But this creature certainly was not friendly—at least, not as human beings understood the word— and neither was it stupid. Unless . . .

He was unable to finish the thought because Berryman had wriggled from beneath the alien and the creature was bouncing up and down between them as it tried furiously to curl and then uncurl its tentacles. Berryman snatched a weapon which was floating nearby and slid it under the being. He pushed it away as Hollis and McCullough let go and the alien went spinning helplessly into the center of the chamber.

"But I wanted to put it with its friends in the

corridor," said Hollis when he had his visor open. "In here, outnumbered five to one, it might panic and injure itself . . ."

"Are you *sure* this air is breathable?" Berryman broke in, speaking through his smashed visor. There was a long incised wound across his nose and one cheek.

"Doctor," said the colonel. "Have a look at Drew's leg. And my shoulder . . ."

"Hollis! Behind you!"

The alien had made contact with the wall net, steadied itself, and then launched itself furiously toward the physicist. Berryman got his ski stick up in time and the alien struck it squarely but did not stop. The butt of the weapon was driven back against the wall, but still the being did not stop. The metal collar piece holding the plate which kept the tip of the weapon from penetrating more than half an inch slipped backward along the shaft. The point, with the alien's considerable velocity and inertia thrown against it, drove into its body until stopped by the interior of its carapace.

It began to slap the shaft of the weapon with its tentacles, violently at first, then more slowly. Suddenly its tentacles tried to tie themselves in knots and it became completely still.

McCullough launched himself toward the alien, knowing that he was in no danger from it now. He gripped one tentacle where it joined the body and gently withdrew the ski stick.

This was much worse than a little property damage or trespass. Much, much worse.

For a long time nobody spoke. McCullough looked slowly around at the other four men, trying desperately not to think. The spacesuits of Morrison,

Drew and Berryman were torn or otherwise rendered useless. The colonel and Drew were injured, perhaps seriously, and, as an added complication, their wounds might well become infected with alien microorganisms—an infection against which their bodies could have no defense. In any case they should be moved out of this place, and quickly. But there were only two usable spacesuits, the physicist's and his own. Hollis' would fit only Hollis. McCullough's might, at a pinch, fit Drew but nobody else. He was afraid to consider all the implications—they were too terrible. But more than anything, he did not want to think about the contorted, alien shape he was holding and the frightful things which must surely happen as a result of its death.

"Doctor," said the colonel in a voice harsh with pain, "you're supposed to know how to treat human beings. Leave that thing alone, it's dead anyway."

He was glad to be able to give his undivided attention to the injured, but somehow the alien cadaver seemed always to be in sight whenever he looked up from a patient, and it became more and more difficult not to think about it. The blood of both species was the same color, a fact which should not have surprised him considering their closely similar atmospheric requirements, and the droplets filled the compartment like dark, frozen rain. The absence of gravity, as well as making it difficult to control bleeding, made it completely impossible to deal quickly with even a simple wound.

Even with the patients cooperating by lacing their arms or feet into the wall netting, and Hollis doing his best to hold McCullough in position while he treated them, it took a long time.

Morrison was in bad shape. An alien had tried to

fasten itself onto his head and chest, but the colonel had been able to interpose his elbow just in time. His forearm was a little longer than the full extension of the alien's horn, so that while his helmet had been hammered into so much scrap metal and his shoulder and upper arm were a mass of punctured and incised wounds, he had escaped with his life. Drew, apparently, had discarded his ski stick in favour of his feet and one leg had suffered in consequence although the injuries were much lighter than the colonel's. Berryman had a badly lacerated face, caused by running it against the edge of his broken visor.

But it was the spacesuits which had suffered worst of all, first from the attacks of the aliens and now at the hands of McCullough.

Cutting and extending the tears in the fabric of the suits, pulling back the plastic and metal foil and the tubing of the air-conditioning systems, affected him much more deeply at times than probing and cleaning the wounds. If they were not already fatally infected the wounds would heal—the human body was self-repairing to a fantastic degree. But increasing the damage to a suit which was not repairable was to inflict a wound of a much more serious nature. In space the suit was much more than a protective skin—Walters, who was in a position to know, had insisted that it was analogous to both womb and placenta, and that losing it prematurely could give rise to a really drastic form of birth trauma.

The thought of being without his own suit in this place was enough to drive McCullough to the edge of panic, and he hated to think of how the others would feel when the shock of their injuries wore off and they realized the full extent of what had happened to them.

His thoughts had taken a Freudian and definitely morbid turn by the time he had finished with them. He found himself staring at the dead body of the Two and wondering if any of them would ever see home again.

The colonel spoke suddenly. His voice sounded very weak and either he was not using his suit radio or the Two's horn had wrecked it. He said, "You will have to report our—our predicament, Doctor. And tell Walters to send the technical material and photographs at the same time. Hollis will have to help you with this—he is the only one of us capable of understanding what we saw in the blister and passing it on. When all this has been done, you will maintain continuous radio contact with us until something has been worked out.

"We will have to move into the corridor while you are leaving," Morrison ended, launching himself slowly toward the inner seal, "so don't waste time."

"It might be better if I stayed," said McCullough awkwardly. "None of you are completely fit, and if they attacked again while you were in the corridor . . ."

"I can't risk losing another spacesuit," said the colonel as he checked his slow light with his feet and good arm. "Drew will organize our defenses. He's very good at that sort of thing."

"And the first thing we do," said Drew savagely, "is take the guards off these stickers! Anything that comes at us again will get six or eight inches of metal in its guts instead of a harmless little jab. Cold steel has a very demoralizing effect on human beings

—that's why bayonet charges have retained their popularity through the ages—and maybe . . ."

"No!" McCullough protested. "We've killed one of them already—by accident, of course—and we can't even imagine the trouble that will cause. But if we start killing them deliberately—I mean, we must all think very carefully about this before we make another move which might be misunderstood."

"And *I* think we've been thinking too much!" Drew said, his voice rising almost to a shout. More quietly he went on, "If a person acts like a wild animal, then that is how he should be treated! And I think we should dump that—that carcass. The damn thing gives me the creeps!"

"While quietly bleeding to death," said Berryman hastily, in an obvious attempt to restore peace, "I have given serious thought to this problem. It seems to me that there are just three things we can do. The first is to return the body to its friends by leaving it in the corridor—a course which might very well anger them even more. The same applies if we keep it in here where they may be able to see it through the lock window. Or lastly, we can hide it from them, with little probability of them ever finding it, by having the doctor and Hollis take it away.

"I favor the last alternative," Berryman concluded, "because, while the aliens may feel fairly certain that it is dead, they cannot be absolutely sure of this—they may assume, or hope, that their friend is a prisoner. If they do not actually see the dead body there might be enough doubt in their minds to make them proceed more cautiously against us."

"My thinking exactly," said the colonel. "Take it to P-Two, Doctor, and find out what makes it tick."

"You have to know your enemy," said Drew viciously, "inside and out."

"Surely you are not suggesting—" began McCullough aghast, then stopped. He was trying hard to think as they must be thinking. *He* had not had his arm and shoulder gored by an alien's horn or had his leg torn by alien claws. *He* was not aware, not as personally and subjectively aware as they were, that his spacesuit was useless with everything which that fact implied. McCullough's skin, and his even more precious spacesuit, was still in one piece. He had been exposed to, but had not suffered, violence.

But violence was a chain reaction with a positive K-factor—once begun it quickly became self-sustaining. From the outset it had been the aliens who had acted violently, or reacted violently, toward the humans. Now the situation had deteriorated to the point where it was becoming uncontrollable because both sides were using violence.

If the aliens reacted violently to the venial sin of trespass, how might they react to one of their people being murdered, and dissected?

chapter twelve

IN THE GENERAL confusion of the past few hours McCullough had forgotten one very important fact, and that was the effect of explosive decompression on an unprotected human or unhuman body. As soon as it was exposed to space, the soft, almost flat underside of the e-t swelled like a great, lumpy football and burst wetly. Nothing he could have done in the way of a post-mortem could have made the alien look worse than it did just then, and by the time he reached P-Two with it he was looking forward to investigating this completely strange life-form.

But there were more urgent matters to be attended to first.

It was not until they had processed the film, and the pictures taken in the blister were on their way pulse by pulse to Earth, that they were fully able to satisfy Walters' curiosity about the fight in the Ship, and then it was only by having him listen while McCullough made his report to Prometheus Control. The physicist, meanwhile, had returned to the Ship with a supply of food and water for Morrison and the others.

Before leaving, Hollis reminded them that the water he was taking would be permanently lost to them, for without the P-ship's reclamation system there was no chance of them being able to use it again. He apologized for mentioning this fact but thought that somebody should bear it in mind in case they were contemplating a lengthy stay.

McCullough agreed and added yet another unpleasant datum to his report.

". . . That is the situation in detail," McCullough said a few minutes later. "Our most urgent need is for spacesuits to evacuate the injured men or, if they cannot be evacuated, food and water to extend our staying time on the Ship until evacuation is possible. There is also the possibility that their wounds may become infected with alien bacteria, against which their bodies may have no defense, and they will die. However, it seems to me that the chances are about even of the alien pathogens running rampant throughout their systems and killing them in a matter of hours, or alternately, of them having no effect whatsoever because the human body is too strange and alien an environment for the e-t pathogens to survive in it. There is also the possibility that our antibiotics will be as effective against e-t infections as they are against . . ."

"Brady here," a voice from Control broke in. It was a gruff, impatient, yet concerned voice belonging to the person on whose shoulders the responsibility for the Prometheus Project and the combined weight of eight stars did not rest lightly. It went on, *"You are in a mess, Doctor, I agree. Have you considered moving one of the P-ships into the lock, taking the*

men on board in shirt-sleeve conditions, leaving one man with a suit to operate the lock mechanism?"

"The lock is too small to take a complete P-ship without wrecking it!" McCullough broke in. "Berryman had that idea, too. But I've already told about it at the beginning of my report."

"If this idea isn't workable," the general was continuing, *"your only hope is to elicit the aid of the alien Ship's crew in getting them out. Are you sure they are as aggressive as you say?"*

"But I've already *told* you—" began McCullough, then stopped. It occurred to him that the distant general was reacting only to the first few sentences of the report, and, as McCullough remembered them, they had not been particularly coherent.

"Stop talking, McCullough, while I'm trying to—" said the general irritably, then in an aside to someone, *"Yes, yes, I'd forgotten the time lag. Now let's see . . . McCullough!"*

"Yes, sir," said McCullough, out of sheer force of habit. Holding conversation with a half-hour delay between each line of dialogue took some getting used to.

Walters, who was tuned to Berryman's suit frequency, said quietly, "The aliens have gone. Both corridor and interhull space are empty. Berryman says their wounds are painful but so far are not unduly inflamed."

"Since the material in your report is urgent and may require a quick decision at any time," the general went on briskly, *"I propose listening with one ear to your report as it comes in while at the same time filling you in on the rather delicate political situation which is developing here. Colonel Morrison is aware of the position as of last night, fifteen hours*

ago, to you, but it has changed since then. It changes
every time you open your mouth, Doctor, and I wish
you would remember that and speak accordingly.

"Briefly, the position is this . . ."

Every transmission made from the area of the
alien Ship had been relayed in its entirety by all the
major networks. The same applied to the pictures
taken during the approach and examination of the
first airlock and the shots McCullough had taken of
the aliens. The reason for such widespread coverage
was simple. Public support and interest in space
flight was on the wane because of the tremendously
expensive hardware needed—especially when pushing out beyond the orbit of Mars—and a blow-by-
blow illustrated account of the first meeting between
humanity and an extraterrestrial culture should re-
vive it if anything could. But now that the meeting
had degenerated into violence, had become literally a
blow-by-blow affair, the idea had backfired.

People were no longer just interested, they were
choosing sides and becoming fanatical.

At first, Prometheus had tried to wrap a security
blanket around the whole incident, but they realized
the uselessness of this when they were reminded that
the P-ships' signals could be received by relatively
unsophisticated equipment, and the stills, although a
little more difficult, required only a moderately sized
radio telescope coupled to the resources of any large
newspaper office.

That was why McCullough was being urged to
choose his words carefully when reporting to Control. If at all possible, he was advised to play down
the seriousness of any given event or development—
the people at Control would realize the true gravity
of the situation and act accordingly, he was assured—

and at all costs avoid displays of fear or anger. It would be an even better practice if McCullough could rehearse his report briefly before transmitting it so as to remove all emotionally loaded words and phrases.

"But *sir*—" began McCullough, then stopped. A picture of Brady sitting in Control drifted in front of his mind's eye to be replaced by one of Berryman, Morrison and Drew frightened and injured and hiding from an alien threat fifty-odd million miles from home, and the thought came to him that Brady must be stupid or he, McCullough, was supposed to be that way. He did not see how their situation could be described in anything but emotionally loaded language without making it sound farcical. If someone was to die, or if the three men in the Ship were to succumb to an alien infection, how was he supposed to report that? As a spot of trouble, perhaps? Or a Bad Show? If the general was really serious in what he had said, McCullough might not be allowed to report a death at all!

"*. . . One good point is that the eavesdropping is strictly one-way. They can hear every word you say but they can't pick up our messages to you. However, I cannot at the moment give you detailed instructions regarding your present situation. Since you are on the spot you must use your own judgment. Just be careful not to . . .*"

While the general was talking, McCullough became aware of another voice in the background—a tiny, harsh, nervous-sounding voice which fought against a constant rattle of interference. He realized suddenly that the voice was his own, speaking the words he had spoken thirty minutes earlier. He could even hear Brady interrupting him again, so that for a few seconds there was one McCullough and two General Bradys talking. It struck him as being wildly funny and he began to laugh.

Walters looked worriedly at him but remained silent. Not so the general.

"... *With the whole world listening to every word you say, you must realize that political capital can be made out of the lightest, unconsidered word. So don't even say Good morning without thinking about it first ...*"

The general went on to say that as the next officer in line of seniority to Colonel Morrison, Lieutenant Colonel McCullough should be prepared at any time to take full control of the expedition. Should casualties occur, should McCullough be forced to assume command, he must be very careful in the matter of wording his reports. The general was not suggesting that he *conceal* the fact that casualties had occurred— he must use his own discretion in this, or perhaps a simple verbal code could be worked out which would allow the communication of sensitive material. The next of kin had the right to know, naturally— but McCullough had no idea how each simple incident at the Ship was being blown up out of all proportion by the news media.

"... *While I don't approve of the emotional frenzy they are whipping up over this, one good point about it is that the supplies you need will be forthcoming. I don't mean to suggest that we would not have sent them anyway even if you did not have the support and sympathy of billions of people, but if you stop to consider how much it will cost to send you just one extra spacesuit, or the price of even a few sips of water ...*"

"If you're *really* worried," said McCullough sarcastically, "we might be able to steal water from the Ship! This would mean us forcing ourselves to overcome a certain—repugnance, shall we say. But have you forgotten that we have an aversion to using even a fellow astronaut's reclaimed water, and for that reason the psychologists insist that our waste fluids are individually recycled . . ."

McCullough broke off. He was supposed to be careful of everything he said and this was, after all, one of the less publicized aspects of space travel . . .

His sarcasm would take just over sixteen minutes to reach General Brady and the same time for the other's reaction to bounce back again. But it seemed suddenly as if the project's chief was telepathic and that thought traveled much faster than light, because Brady went on apologetically, *"We are not counting the pennies on this, however, or even the millions of dollars, so there is no reason for concern over this aspect of the situation. Just take it easy, do your best and, before you open your mouth, remember all those listening millions who are ready to jump to wrong conclusions.*

"And now we will consider the matter of urgent supplies.

"These will reach you via a modified high-acceleration probe in forty-one days—a five-day countdown, which has already started, and thirty-six days for the trip. We will discuss rendezvous procedure later. Right now I must tell you that the payload is an integral part of the vehicle and ask that you give urgent thought to its composition. Should priority be given to food, water, replacement spacesuits, weapons and in what proportion?

"No doubt you will want to talk about this with

the men on the Ship, so I'll sign off now. Good luck to all of you."

The general was followed by a McDonnell man who talked endlessly about the weight and size limitations of their supply vehicle and the rendezvous problems. McCullough left Walters to listen to him while he relayed a shortened version of Brady's instructions to the men in the Ship. He spoke to Drew because everyone else was asleep. Drew did not want to wake the colonel and McCullough agreed that the matter could wait for a few hours. But the mention of sleep made him pause for a moment to calculate how long it had been since he had had any, and the immediate result of his calculations was a jaw-wrenching yawn. He told Drew that Walters, Hollis and he would stand radio watch in turn while the others caught up on their sleep, and asked to be called if there was the slightest change in the condition of their wounds, or any other emergency.

Hollis returned while he was talking. As if his arrival was the cue, a dry, pedantic voice replaced that of the McDonnell man. From the physicist's expression McCullough knew that questions of a highly specialized and technical nature were about to be directed at Hollis. He wanted to avoid another delayed-action dialogue starting up while they were all so tired, so he broke in to say that they all needed rest and would resume contact, unless there was a sudden emergency, in twelve hours.

To Walters and Hollis he suggested—McCullough did not feel comfortable about giving orders, despite his technically superior rank—that they get some rest while he stood first watch.

The physicist nodded and began struggling out of his suit prior to strapping in. Walters, who was already strapped into his couch, linked fingers behind his neck and elaborately closed his eyes. Shortly afterward the pilot was asleep and Hollis had his eyes closed, pretending. He was scratching surreptitiously at the side of his neck turned away from McCullough. Despite himself, the doctor felt his own eyes closing.

Obviously he was going to need something more strenuous than worrying about the physicist's mental health to keep him awake, and his first thought was the investigation of the alien cadaver. But he could not work here—it would be stretching even Walters' sense of humor to the breaking point if the pilot was to wake up to find the module filled with drifting alien entrails—and the lock where he had left the specimen was too cramped. The best thing would be for him to move to P-Two's command module, which he would have all to himself, and use the other ship's radio to listen for trouble developing at the bridgehead.

After listening to Brady and Drew, he thought irritably, *even I'm beginning to think like a general!*

But as his examination of the e-t proceeded, McCullough's tiredness was forgotten. He had begun by assuming that the alien's vital organs, including its brain, would be housed high under the protective carapace and his assumption proved correct. He was able to identify and isolate the lungs, the odd-looking muscular pump which was the heart, and the mechanism of ingestion, digestion and excretion. At each major step in the examination he took photographs.

There were puzzles at first, but one by one they were solved as he charted the digestive, respiratory and, so far as he was able with the instruments available to him, the nervous system. Tracing the connections to the eyes, ears and to the vicious weapon projecting from its underside was relatively easy—the thing was simply a curved horn with a small degree of mobility and not, as he had at first thought, a sting. But there were a few puzzles which refused to be solved. The being's reproductive system was a completely closed book to him. He had no idea what sort of environment could cause a creature shaped as this one was to evolve, and there were points which bothered him about angles of vision and the degree of control the being exercised over all four tentacles. There was no evidence of specialization in any of the appendages.

He wondered if ambidextrous was the right word to use for a being with four hands, but he was too weary to solve that puzzle as well. He began to tidy away the grisly pieces of alien which floated about the command module, thinking that he would have to waken Walters so that he, McCullough, would have a chance to sleep on his many problems.

But when he did go to sleep there were no solutions waiting to rise out of his subconscious. Instead he dreamed only of Berryman, Morrison and Drew and of the nightmarish fates which could befall them, culminating in one which involved a fungus growing out of their wounds and spreading over their whole bodies until they became great, livid, mobile sponges which mewed and gobbled appealingly at him while they chased him along the bright, net-covered corridors of the alien Ship.

That one woke him up screaming.

chapter thirteen

Six days went by and none of the men on the Ship died or even became infected. Perhaps their bodies were too alien an environment for extraterrestrial microorganisms to survive in them, or it may have been that Earth medication and antibiotics were a match for most germs regardless of origin. McCullough's pleasure and relief over this was intense, but the feeling was banished shortly afterward by his row with the general.

McCullough had evolved a number of theories about the alien Type Two, but he wanted to have his conclusions regarding some of the more puzzling aspects of its physiology vetted by someone more eminent in the field. He had prepared, and had Walters transmit, a group of eight photographs taken during the alien's post-mortem before commencing his verbal report, and in the thousand-odd seconds it took for the signal to reach Earth and for the general's first reaction to come back, he said quite a lot.

Too much, obviously.

"Silence! Stop talking at once!" Brady's voice roared at him suddenly. *"For God's sake STOP TALKING!"*

But so far as the general was concerned, there was nothing that could stop McCullough's voice arriving for at least another half hour, and Brady quickly realized this. He was still angry but his tone became almost resigned as he went on, *"You are supposed to be very careful of every word you say, McCullough. If you do or say anything wrong, it reflects on all of us. Not just on you people out there or on the project personnel, our whole country and its ideology suffers as a consequence! Don't you realize that what you've just done will cause a storm of criticism and censure from inside as well as outside the country, that a large section of the world's population is going to feel angry and ashamed of what you have done out there?*

"Every time you open your mouth, McCullough, you lose friends and we lose support! Think, dammit, before you talk!

"There are some who will be pleased with what you are doing," the general went on bitterly. *"The biologists who are too interested in finding out what makes an alien tick to think of ethical and political side effects. And there are the various groups advocating that a stronger line should be taken against these unfriendly aliens. But even you must be aware of how much trouble is caused by people who object to dissection practiced on domestic animals and pets, and now YOU have to start cutting up a member of an intelligent extraterrestrial species!"*

And so it went on.

McCullough remained silent with a considerable effort. A lot had happened during the six days since the fight with the aliens. From Earth the first high-acceleration supply vehicle had been launched, proceeded, accompanied and followed by thousands of words of cautious advice. In P-Two McCullough had completed his examination of the alien and had passed his thoughts about it to the three men marooned on the Ship. His chief reason for doing this had been to give them something else to think about other than their wounds—wounds from which they had not really expected to recover. But now that recovery was simply a matter of time, it was a little embarrassing for McCullough that his theory had been accepted in toto by everyone but himself.

The reason for that, of course, was that it made them feel less guilty over some of the things they had done.

But it was, after all, only a theory, and the facts on which it was based could be interpreted several ways. McCullough had transmitted a group of pictures and a number of verbal facts before the general had started having hysterics. He had not even mentioned his theory. Apparently Brady did not want to hear it. Brady did not want to hear *anything*!

"Doctor," said Walters in a whisper. "You've been tapping that mike with your finger for the past ten minutes. When the general gets around to hearing it he will think something terrible is happening."

"Something is," said McCullough. "I'm losing my patience."

He paused, then choosing his words with great care, went on, "Since I am forbidden to discuss my findings on the Type Two alien's physiology, or draw conclusions from them or even ask questions regarding them from people who are more knowledgeable than myself, there is nothing more to say except this. The photographs and verbal report transmitted so far represent facts, and both my theory and the questions arising from it are implicit in these facts if you bring them to the attention of the right people. Message ends."

The general was still complaining bitterly. McCullough tuned him down to a whisper and knocked off the transmit switch. He picked up the length of modified tubing Walters and he had been working on, then told the pilot that he was going to the Ship and that he would send Hollis back as soon as he arrived there. If the general or any lesser light from Control wanted to hear from them, they should talk about hyperdrive generators and nothing else.

He entered the lock chamber a few minutes later and Hollis left it, closing the outer seal behind him. Immediately there was a rush of air entering from the corridor which was quickly followed by the three marooned men. Even though there were no aliens outside the chamber, the men's movements were fast, precise and economical—a complex, well practiced drill. Outwardly at least, they were adapting to conditions inside the Ship. Before McCullough could speak, Drew dived toward him, checked himself expertly against a lashing point and said, "Is that the new weapon?"

McCullough nodded and with obvious reluctance handed it over.

"I know how you feel, Doctor," said Drew. "You are worried about this new form of frightfulness you are about to unloose on our little world. But this isn't a mass-destruction weapon. We will be discriminating in its use and kill only aliens who are trying to kill us . . ."

"But they are aliens!" said McCullough angrily. "My theory could be completely wrong."

"I think not," said Colonel Morrison, joining them. "In any case we are badly in need of a Two-stopper, and it looks as if you've given us one."

When a Two was stabbed with one of the existing spears it was still possible for it to inflict considerable damage before it died, so the weapon had been shortened slightly so as to make it handle like a sword. At the business end the tubing had been cut diagonally in the manner of a hypodermic needle and the tip flattened and given a razor edge on both sides. A few inches back from the tip, the blade curved through an angle of about thirty degrees so that it looked a little like a bullfighter's sword.

The effect would be to inflict a deep-punctured wound, after which the damage could be multiplied and compounded by giving the weapon a quick, semicircular twist before tugging it free. The thought of the frightful internal devastation a properly delivered thrust and twist would inflict on the victim's body made McCullough feel physically as well as mentally uncomfortable. He was still not sure how he had become a party to this thing.

Hippocrates and Asclepius, he thought, would not have approved of his behavior in this matter.

His only real excuse for producing the weapon was an unsatisfactory one even to himself, the fact that the Two's horn was also a cruel and deadly instrument of destruction. There was also the fact that the damage the new weapon would inflict on vital organs, the massive hemorrhaging it would cause, would paralyze the alien with shock and cause death within a few seconds, so that in a way it was almost humane.

The colonel's voice broke in on his thoughts, giving him a welcome change of mental subject. Morrison said, "What I really want to know is how much freedom of action I am allowed. Can we use our own initiative regarding the local situation and the problems rising out of it, or must all our thinking be done from the Cape?"

"Our thinking is being done," said McCullough with a deliberate lack of inflection in his voice, "by the Russians, the Buddhists, the United Nations, and the Society for the Prevention of Cruelty to Animals."

They were all watching him.

Morrison's shoulder and arm were still giving him pain, McCullough knew, and the other two were by no means comfortable. They had all lost a good deal of blood and been under constant strain with inadequate sleep since being marooned on the Ship. The bright-blue lighting made it impossible to conceal subtle changes of expression or variations of facial pallor. They were all staring at him so intently that the thought uppermost in his mind must have been plain for all of them to see.

I want to go home!

"Go on, Doctor," said Morrison harshly.

"Very well, sir," said McCullough. "Our problem, or rather *your* problem, is this. We are being told what to do by people who do not know all the facts, and who don't want to be told them because of the effect the telling might have on public opinion. Their instructions to us, if you could call them instructions, are so general in nature and so hedged around with qualifiers and warnings that they don't really seem to mean anything. We need help. Not only are we not getting it, we are being ordered not to ask for it!

"I, personally, would like corroboration of my findings in the Two autopsy," McCullough went on, anger gradually replacing the fear in his voice. "Moral support, if you like, for a theory and a decision I am too much a coward to take alone. Instead of giving me the necessary support, Brady nearly had a fit and would not let me finish explaining the situation! I don't know what has happened to them back there. They act as if *they* are having an emergency instead of us!"

"In a sense, they are—" began Morrison.

"I think you're being too unselfish, sir," said McCullough bitingly. "It is my considered professional opinion, for which I do *not* need moral support, that the mental and physical stresses involved in coping with the local situation are severe enough without also making us responsible for possible changes in the political situation at home.

"The whole idea is ridiculous! We are in the limelight as no other group of men has ever been, we know this. In a sense we may be standing trial for our whole race. But our work here will be more valuable, or reactions more honest if you like, if we don't allow ourselves to be paralyzed with stage fright!

"I would like permission, sir," McCullough ended less vehemently, "to request information and assistance from Control without having to consider mass audience reactions."

"You have a point, Doctor," said Morrison, after a short pause. "At the same time, we can't afford to ignore public opinion completely."

"But that's the way Brady talks!"

"I'll think about it, Doctor," said Morrison sharply. "Right now we must discuss the food and water situation, weapons, tactics and—and a change of base. While we are here we may as well find out as much as possible about the Ship. And while we're talking, Doctor, I'd like you to look at my dressings."

McCullough wondered if the colonel was looking for sympathy, then immediately felt ashamed for thinking such a thing. Morrison's injury was painful and inflamed, although not infected, and it was only one of his many problems. For his physical impairment had seriously undermined his authority. With one arm virtually useless he was dependent on his inferior officers not only for protection but for the kind of assistance which was more common in a nurse-patient relationship. And cut off as he was from direct contact with Control, he could no longer speak with all the authority of Earth behind his words. As well, the project which he headed had come thoroughly unstuck.

At the present moment the colonel must be feeling frightened and impotent and pretty much a total loss to himself and everyone else, and as a doctor, McCullough should not be aggravating these feelings.

It was a time for applying oil to the situation, or perhaps butter. Not broken glass.

McCullough stayed on the Ship three days. In that time their 'bridgehead' was moved twice, on both occasions to compartments close to the generator blister so as to facilitate the work of Hollis. Despite the Twos which attacked them at frequent but irregular intervals, and at times kept them pinned down in their base for hours on end, the work of gathering information about the Ship went on.

When friction developed, which was frequently, he applied oil. McCullough was sure that his bedside manner had never had such a strenuous workout in all its long life. But his charm did not work very well on the colonel. Despite his arguments on the necessity of gathering further data either to support or disprove his theory, Morrison would not allow him to attempt communication with the Twos.

Twos, the colonel had said . . .

chapter fourteen

DURING HIS NEXT report to the general, McCullough's voice was as neutral and unemotional as any human voice could be—to begin with, anyway.

"In the light of additional data gathered within the past few days," he said carefully, "we may have to modify our thinking considerably regarding the purpose of the alien Ship and its crew.

"First, the Ship . . ."

The alien vessel had made a controlled approach and had been inserted into an orbit which showed every indication of being precalculated, McCullough went on, after which it had taken no action of any kind. This, however, did not preclude the possibility that it was gathering data, since the forward section contained a number of transparent protective blisters which might very well house sensory equipment of some kind. In fact, the primary—perhaps the only—purpose of the Ship was the gathering of such data.

Where the Ship's construction was concerned—

and here McCullough had to admit that they had investigated only a very small fraction of the vessel's enormous volume—they had come to certain fairly definite conclusions.

The way they now saw it, the Ship's construction was based on a design philosophy in which weight was of little or no importance. Apparently its source of power was so efficient that there was no necessity to save an ounce or a pound here and there by putting lightening holes in structural members or designing down an angle bracket so that it would take only the amount of stress necessary to its function plus a fractional safety overlap.

All the indications pointed to the fact that the Ship had been built in space, probably in an extrasolar asteriod belt or close to a small moon where metal and the means of working it were to hand. The more sophisticated power, control and life-support systems had almost certainly been built on the home planet and transported piecemeal to the hull. What little they had seen of the layout of corridors, wall nets and numerous access points to the Ship's interior made them certain that all this had been designed to facilitate the vessel's builders rather than its crew.

They may have been guilty of grossly overestimating the intelligence and capabilities of the crews as well.

"We have complete data on only one of these three life-forms," McCullough went on, "and that is the tentacled, starfish-shaped Type Two. During all our meetings with them these beings have been completely and uniformly aggressive, so much so that after the second alien attack, Drew remarked that if they behaved like wild animals they should be treated as such. My subsequent physiological investigation of the Two revealed a brain structure and nervous system which appeared unusually small and uncomplicated, and a lack of fine control in the appendages, facts which supported Drew's theory.

"We are all now of the opinion that we have been trying to establish intelligent communication with the alien equivalent of guinea pigs!"

Their current theory was that the Ship was an interstellar probe of some kind carrying experimental animals which had escaped and overrun the Ship and killed its crew. There was also a strong possibility that it did not, and had never had, a crew, and that the life-support system and internal lighting was initially for use during the vessel's construction and was subsequently being used by the animal passengers. This being the case, they felt free to fight a defensive war against the alien life-forms infesting the Ship while they mapped, photographed and learned everything they could about the vessel's equipment and function.

Priority, however, would be given to finding a method of patching-in to the alien life-support system. The reason for this, as had been already explained, was that the water used by the marooned men was almost completely lost since only a fraction was recoverable to be put through the P-ship's recycling system.

"Our water is being carefully rationed," McCullough continued, "and at the present rate of consumption the supply will last for thirty-two days. This will take us three days past the arrival time of the supply vehicle, but *it* will carry only a forty-day supply of water! A few minutes simple computation will show that unless we can return the marooned men to the

P-ships where the water supply can be recycled properly, our supply problem is logistically insoluble.

"We have already drawn heavily on the food meant for the return trip," McCullough ended grimly, "and if we don't find a local source of water we can never come home."

About the only thing McCullough did not have to worry about was General Brady's reaction to this latest report. Earth and Prometheus Control were only a few weeks off the time when they would pass behind the sun, the relay vehicle designed to circumvent this difficulty was not yet in operation, and incoming messages were rendered almost unintelligible by interference.

Not completely unintelligible, of course. By asking Control to repeat every sentence anything up to ten times, Walters was usually able to piece together a complete message. Unlike McCullough, however, Walters had nothing better to do, and somehow a signal lost a good deal of its urgency and emotional content when it had to be repeated so many times.

Precisely on time the high-acceleration supply rocket homed-in on P-One's beacon and was taken aboard the alien Ship. It contained, in addition to the promised water, a twenty-day supply of food, film, paper, and a collapsed, carefully packed spacesuit. Some well-wisher had tucked a .45 automatic inside the spacesuit, probably on impulse and without taking time to think about packing it properly, and the forty-G acceleration of the supply vehicle had caused the heavy gun to tear a large hole in the hip and leg sections, rendering the suit completely useless.

They had lost a spacesuit and gained an automatic pistol for which there was no ammunition.

Their search pattern took the form of a flat spiral which wound slowly around the lateral axis of the Ship while moving even more slowly forward. At regular intervals a temporary base was set up with a search radius of twenty-five yards or more, depending on the available accommodation and the hostility and numbers of the local population. When completed, the search pattern would still leave a long, empty core of unexplored territory in the three-dimensional map they were constructing.

They found only storerooms and compartments, packed with equipment whose shapes and purpose were slowly becoming familiar to them, and the ever-present netted corridors linking them together. It seemed obvious that the crew's quarters, if any, the life-support system and other essential services were deep in the as yet unexplored center of the Ship.

"It is very bad tactics to cut ourselves off from the outer hull and contact with our ships," said the colonel as they paused, between sorties, to fill in another small section of their map, "but it seems to me that there are certain periods when the risk is lessened. You must all have noticed the regular decrease in alien activity and numbers which seems to occur every five or six hours. If we assume this to be due to periodic feeding, we can, at these times, push the search deeper into the Ship. Or we might try following some of the e-t's—at a safe distance, of course—in the hope of their leading us to the source of the food and water."

Hollis said, "The absence of e-t's is not entirely regular, sir. There seems to be a longer absence,

possibly due to a sleep period, between every few
meals. This could be an important datum in calculat-
ing the length of their day and the rotation of their
home planet."

"Personally," said Drew impatiently, "I am more
interested in gathering data which will aid our survival. For instance, if one of us should lose his
weapon, is there enough known about their physical
makeup for us to use an e-t form of karate on them?
Or put another way, Doctor, where is the dirtiest
spot I can plant my boot?"

Reluctantly, McCullough told him.

They did not deliberately try to kill the aliens,
doing so only when the Twos attacked them—which
was always. Once they came on a dead Two whose
condition suggested that it had been partially eaten.
This was another important datum, Hollis said,
which gave strong support to McCullough's theory
that the e-t's were experimental animals running wild
rather than sentient beings.

This did not comfort McCullough as much as it
should have done, because he was developing a new
theory. It rested on the premise that the Ship had
suffered some kind of nonmaterial catastrophe—the
psychological pressures of a too lengthy voyage, perhaps—which had driven the crew insane so that the
Twos were either the survivors or descendants of the
original personnel now reduced to little more than
animals.

But he did not mention his new theory to the
others because it would have made them unhappy
and uncertain again.

Hollis and Berryman were becoming expert at
identifying and tracing power and control lines without actually knowing what it was the lines powered

or controlled. It should be possible, they insisted, to utilize one of these currently dead circuits to carry radio messages from deep inside the Ship to the metal of the outer hull. In effect the circuit or section of plumbing would be an extension of their suit antennae and, since the signals would be in the form of radio frequency impulses rather than a flow of current, there was little danger of them inadvertently switching on one of the alien controls or mechanisms.

In order to test this idea and also to get a line on the whereabouts of the Twos' feeding place, the next base was established some forty yards inboard.

It was a large, gray-walled compartment filled with disciplined masses of plumbing and the usual sealed cabinets growing out from all six sides. A quick search showed it to be empty, and McCullough guarded the only entrance, which was a sliding door rather than the airtight seals found under the hull area. Hollis, Berryman and Drew were bunched together with Morrison floating close by, when they started to argue about a Two they had killed and whether they had defended themselves before or after it had actually attacked. They began talking loudly, vehemently, obviously feeling safe in this bright alien cupboard, when the Two which had been hiding somewhere in the compartment landed among them.

There were shouts, curses and a scream that jerked on and off regularly, as if someone was trying to hold a high note while his back was being clapped. McCullough swung round and raised his weapon, but the center of the room was a confused mass of twisting, struggling bodies which were rapidly becoming obscured by a growing red fog and there was nothing he could do. The Two had wrapped its tentacles around someone and was furiously disembowelling him with its horn while the others tried to tear it loose and kick and stab it to death.

When they finally succeeded in pulling it away, McCullough launched himself toward the man, grabbed him around the waist and held him tightly face to face so that he would not be able to see his terrible wounds. Then he told the man lies in a gentle, reassuring voice until Drew separated them, saying harshly that the colonel was dead.

Berryman, Hollis and Drew were watching him, obviously waiting for instructions, or possibly for some indication that he was unwilling to accept his responsibility. McCullough squeezed his eyes shut in an attempt to obliterate the sight of Morrison's body from his mind's eye as well as from normal vision. He tried to picture the colonel alive, as he had been a few days or hours ago, but great soft balls of coagulating blood like tacky grapes drifted against his face as a reminder that all images of Morrison alive would inevitably lead to the one he was trying to blot out of Morrison dead. It was impossible for McCullough to think of the colonel without seeing the grisly thing which spun slowly beside him like a bloody Catherine wheel. Because it had once been Morrison it inhabited every second of the past as well as the present. It was only in the future that the colonel did not really exist.

There was a feverish sort of logic about that thought, McCullough told himself. He must think only of a time when the colonel did not exist, and avoid bringing up memories of him; he must think only of the future. But there were a number of futures and they began flickering past his mind's eye like pictures from the Black Museum. A drowning man was supposed to see his past life passing before his eyes, but McCullough was seeing an endless succession of future deaths, so he opened his eyes and stared back at the others.

He said, "Berryman, find an empty tool locker or something and put the colonel's body in it. Wire or wedge the fastening so's those animals won't be able to get at him. When you've finished, go to the nearest hull lock chamber and report what has happened to Walters. Today we planned to follow the Twos to their food and water supply and that is still at the top of our list of priorities.

"However," he concluded, "if you hear a disturbance, don't come charging to our rescue. Stay in a safe place until the next lunch break and then make your way back here. Understand?"

Berryman looked from Hollis to Drew and then back to McCullough. Despite the differences in rank and the military discipline which was supposed to bind them, this, McCullough knew, was something in the nature of an election. From his expression it was obvious that Hollis was voting a timid positive, Drew's features registered an angry negative, and Walter's opinions, since he was no longer directly involved in the Two-human running battle which was being waged in the Ship, were not being considered. It was Berryman, therefore, who had the casting vote in this election, and while the silence dragged on, McCullough wondered what qualities this normally lighthearted pilot thought important in a leader, and if his qualifications were insufficient, how exactly Berryman would let him know about it.

He would be an extremely tactful and kindly mutineer, McCullough thought.

Finally Berryman nodded and said drily, "The Colonel is dead. Long live the Lieutenant Colonel ..."

It had been Morrison's intention to probe the Ship as deeply as possible today, and to follow the aliens to their feeding place despite the risk of the Earth party ending up being surrounded by practically every Two in the Ship. McCullough's instructions were not unexpected, and they probably thought he was carrying on as planned out of respect for their dead colonel, or if they were feeling cynical, because he could think of nothing better to do.

As he led them into the corridor, McCullough wondered why it was so important to him that he should get as far away from the colonel's body as possible. In the past he had treated automobile accident cases and examined the pulverized remains of jet pilots who had hit the deck at close to Mach One, so that Morrison's body was not by any means the worst sight he had had to witness in his life. He had even seen a matador gored repeatedly by a bull on one occasion, and while he had felt clinical concern for the unfortunate man, some detached portion of his mind—a group of rebel brain cells, perhaps, which had abstained when the majority were taking the Hippocratic Oath—had been glad that on this occasion the bull had been able to hit back. It was just that in some obscure fashion the colonel's had been such a dirty death, and McCullough did not want to think about it at all.

They spotted a Two about ten minutes later and trailed it at a distance of twenty yards or less, depending on the turns and twists of its route. At intervals they wrapped pieces of paper around the netting so that they would be able to find their way back again. But the Two ignored them, either because it did not see them or because it had something more important on its mind. A few minutes later it was joined by another of its kind, then three more, none of which showed any interest in their pursuers. The men were pushing deeper and deeper into the Ship now, and large stretches of the corridors were permanently lit—they did not have to switch on the corridor lighting here and could not even see the switches which controlled it. They also became aware of a low, moaning sound which rose and fell and changed pitch constantly but erratically and grew steadily louder as they went on.

Suddenly there were three aliens following them and gaining steadily. Before they became sandwiched too tightly between the two groups of e-t's, McCullough led his party into the next empty compartment. Its sliding door had a large window so he did not switch on the room lights. While waiting for the second group to pass he had a few minutes to look around, and he discovered something which almost made him call off the search for a water supply.

This compartment was different from the others they had examined. Even the light which filtered in from the corridor made that very plain. The cable runs and ducting were absent or hidden behind flush wall panels and the objects occupying the room had the unmistakable, finished look of items of furniture. In the center of the room there was suspended a long, cylindrical shape which could very well be a free-fall hammock.

"They've gone past," said Drew, opening the sliding door. "We'll have to hurry—they're turning into an intersection . . ."

Very carefully McCullough marked the position of the compartment on his map, then left with the others. He still felt that he should have made them stop until they had examined and considered all the implications of the room they had just left.

A lab animal would not require a furnished room, which meant that there were intelligent extraterrestrials on the Ship.

He needed time to think. The search for water could be postponed for a few hours or days while they decided what was the best thing to do. McCullough was the boss and he would order a return to base.

But McCullough did not give the order because everything began happening at once.

They turned into a corridor unlike any they had seen before. One wall was made up of heavy wire mesh through which they could see a large compartment filled with Twos, while other Twos fought and wriggled their way through gaps in the mesh. Inside the enclosure the fighting and jockeying for position was so vicious that several of the e-t's were dead. The object of the fighting seemed to be to gain a position near a long plastic panel running along one wall of the enclosure. From the panel there sprouted a large number of open, small-diameter pipes and a similar number which terminated in rubbery swellings. The fighting which was going on made it difficult to see exactly what it was that was oozing out of them.

"Semiliquid food from the pipes, I think," said Hollis excitedly, "and what looks like water from the nipples!"

He broke off as a single, deafening chime reverberated along the corridor and they heard their first alien voice.

It could have been his imagination, but McCullough felt sure that the sound was subtly unlike the alien gobblings of the Twos. The word-sounds seemed more complex and meaningful somehow, and there was almost a quality of urgency about them. He knew that it was ridiculous to read meanings into a completely alien sequence of sounds, but his feeling of being warned remained strong. Each time the voice paused, the single, tremendous chime was repeated—or perhaps the voice was speaking quickly between chimes.

The Twos on the other side of the mesh became more agitated when a chime sounded, but they did not stop either eating or fighting each other.

Drew said something about Pavlov to Hollis and McCullough unstrapped his tape recorder. Drew swung his weapon to point at a nearby speaker grill where it would be possible to get a recording without too much interference from the feeding animals, but he never completed the movement. There was a blinding double flash as the spear touched the mesh and the corridor. Drew jerked violently, then became motionless except for a slow, lateral spin.

A second alien voice joined the first one and the moaning sounds increased in intensity.

The new voice seemed to be speaking the same language. Very often it repeated the same word-sounds as the first voice, but it spoke over or around it and did not pause for the chimes. Sometimes it spoke quickly and at other times the words were dragged out and their pitch, volume and inflection varied so widely that it seemed to be trying to sing.

McCullough felt confused and stupid as he blinked away the green afterimage of the flash and tried to make some kind of sense out of what was happening. He needed time to think.

But he was given no time to think, because Berryman was coming back and shouting at them from the other end of the corridor.

"Doctor! *Doctor!* Walters says the generator blisters are beginning to glow—all of them that he can see from P-Two! *He says the Ship is leaving!*"

chapter fifteen

FOR THE FIRST few seconds McCullough's feeling was one of outrage rather than fear. This was going too far, he thought; being marooned on the Ship, running short of water, under nearly constant attack by aliens, the deaths of Colonel Morrison and Drew. This was piling on the agony and taking misfortune to ridiculous extremes. The Ship *couldn't* be leaving!

But Berryman kept babbling on about Walters and the glow enamating from the interior of the transparent generator blisters and the interference which was being picked up by P-Two's radio, all of which indicated a steady build-up of power within the Ship. Then there was the constant gabbling of the Twos, the chiming, the alien voices and moaning sound pouring out of the wall speaker. If the Ship was leaving, McCullough would be expected to do something about it, react in some fashion, make decisions, give orders *now*.

He couldn't.

The problem was too big and complicated for

quick decisions and inspired leadership—at least, so far as he was concerned. He had to put it into some sort of order in his mind, take time to consider the events in consecutive fashion and break the problem down, even though they might have no time at all. He must go back past Berryman's arrival to the time when Drew was alive and only the alien voices . . .

McCullough's mind came to a sudden halt at that point and ground into reverse. Drew might very well be still alive. Now that he had time to think about it, the more likely it became. He pointed at the mesh and at Drew and tried to speak.

What he wanted to say was that the mesh was electrified and they should stay clear of it, and that Drew's weapon had touched it while the haft was in contact with the floor, so that the flash had been a short along the shaft of the spear. He wanted to tell them that in his opinion the mesh was not too highly charged—the way he saw it there should be just enough kick in it to keep the captive animals under control—and in any case Drew had been wearing his suit gauntlets which would give added protection. Considering the gauntlets and the fact that the discharge had gone through the weapon and not by way of Drew's body, he tried to say, there was a good chance that prompt resuscitation measures would save him. But all he could do was stammer and point. He could not make them understand or even hold their attention.

Hollis shouted something at him but a chime from the speaker a few inches from McCullough's ear kept him from hearing what the physicist had said. But Berryman was closer to Hollis and replied. Hollis pulled Drew's weapon out of the air and added it to the one already in his hand, shouted something at

McCullough, then launched himself back in the direction from which they had just come. Berryman looked from the physicist's fast-disappearing feet to McCullough and back again, waved and bellowed.

It had been impossible to hear what either of them had been saying over the cacophony of chimes, moaning, squabbling Twos and the alien duet.

McCullough could understand Hollis running away. The physicist was wearing one of the two remaining undamaged spacesuits and there was a chance that he could make it to the airlock and to the P-ships in time. But why was the pilot running away? Surely Berryman did not think that he could take Hollis' suit away from him, after fighting him for it and knocking him unconscious? The only result of such a fight would be another ruptured spacesuit.

Not knowing what to think and feeling bitterly disappointed in both of them, McCullough opened his visor and dived slowly toward Drew. In the weightless condition and with an electrified mesh just a few feet away, there was only one method of resuscitation possible. McCullough did his best to ignore the alien voices rattling at him from the speaker, the gobbles and wheezing sounds coming from the Twos and the all-pervading moaning and chiming, and concentrated instead on administering the Kiss of Life to the dead or unconscious Drew.

But finding Drew's mouth was like ducking for apples in a tub of water at Halloween. The pilot's head kept bobbing away and rolling flabbily about inside his helmet. Finally, by sliding one hand carefully into the helmet and supporting the back of Drew's neck with his fingers, McCullough was able to press the other's face forward into the visor opening.

Results came quickly after that.

Gasping and choking and struggling like a drowning man, Drew began to come to. He flung one arm around McCullough's neck so tightly that the doctor thought his helmet would come off and possibly his head as well. He was able to hold Drew clear of the electrified mesh until the pilot settled down, then he detached the arm from around his neck.

For some reason McCullough was feeling unusually well disposed toward the pilot. Possibly this was because he might have been instrumental in saving the other's life and this made him feel a vaguely godlike possessiveness and concern for this life he might have saved. As well, there was the fact that Drew would be the only company available if the other two did not come back. And after everything the pilot had been through he did not want to add to Drew's troubles by telling him that the Ship was leaving, even though every instinct he possessed seemed to be urging him to get to the nearest airlock and jump for the P-ships while he had the chance.

Drew was mumbling something at him, looking very awkward and embarrassed.

Obviously the chimes and alien voices were some kind of pre-takeoff warning. While they continued there was still a chance for him to leave the Ship.

"I can't hear you," he said hurriedly to the pilot. "But there's no need to thank me—you probably wouldn't have died anyway . . ."

"You mustn't think I meant it personally," Drew broke in, speaking loudly but with his awkwardness still very much in evidence. "It was just that your hand and your mouth . . . I mean, there was a girl at home who—who ... For a minute I thought ... Dammit, Doc, I don't want you thinking I'm some kind of pervert or anything!"

Get out of here! screamed a voice in McCullough's mind, while another pointed out the ridiculous, almost insane humor of the situation and urged him to laugh while yet another voice, calmer and more clinical, reminded him that so far as Drew was concerned this was a very serious matter and he should avoid hurting the pilot's feelings.

"The thought," said McCullough with the ring of absolute truth and sincerity in his voice, "never entered my mind. But if you look in the enclosure you'll see the Twos are beginning to lose interest in their feeding. We had better leave before they see us."

"What happened to my spear?" said Drew. "Where are Hollis and Berryman? It is very bad tactics to split up our force like this, sir ..."

Drew was his old self again, obviously, and McCullough felt less hesitation about passing on the bad news of the Ship leaving and the desertion of Hollis and Berryman. But he was saved the trouble. Berryman was with them again, hanging onto the wall net and trying to talk and catch his breath at the same time.

He was giving Drew a startled, I-didn't-expect-to-see-you-alive-again sort of look while he spoke to McCullough. He said, "Sorry for leaving you—without permission—just now. I got excited and took off—without thinking. When you gave Captain Hollis the idea for—for shorting the generator with the metal spears—he told me he needed help. He still does, inside the blister. You have the only other working spacesuit, sir. We haven't much time ..."

Until then McCullough had not been aware that he had given an idea to anyone, but he realized at once what Hollis was trying to do because they had discussed just this eventuality several times. In general, that was—he would have to wait until they reached the generator blister to see what particular form of sabotage the physicist had been able to devise.

On the way they surprised a not quite fully grown Two at an intersection. Being unarmed, Drew and Berryman grabbed two tentacles each, twisted their feet into the wall net, and swung it hard and repeatedly against a projecting bracket until its carapace split and it stopped moving. Berryman looked slightly sick and Drew, who had devised this particular method of unarmed combat, muttered something about neatness and dispatch.

McCullough wondered why such complimentary terms were used to describe such a vicious and despicable act. But with every wall speaker erupting chimes and a continuous alien gabble bounding their ears; with the knowledge that all around them the generators which could whisk them away to some alien solar system were building up to full power, it was impossible to behave in an ethical and moral manner. It was impossible, McCullough thought cynically, because so very few human beings were capable of such behavior in the present circumstances, and if enough people considered it impossible, then it was impossible.

For four frightened astronauts, read fifty million Frenchmen who could not be wrong, and for fifty million Frenchmen, read the whole human race . . .

For a moment the thought came to him of traveling an unguessable number of light-years to another solar system, of seeing an alien world and its culture and having contact with true, extraterrestrial intelligences—even if only briefly as an animal they might consider of too little interest or importance to keep alive. The idea of not helping the physicist, of ordering Hollis to cease attempting to sabotage the generator, came and was hurriedly rejected. The sudden, awful wonder of his original thought was quickly overwhelmed by fear.

They passed quickly through the lock chamber and the interhull space where their first major brush with the Twos had occurred, and on to the lock which gave access to the generator blister. Hollis' legs showed in the transparent panel of the inner seal.

As McCullough was joining him, Berryman placed his antenna against the bulkhead and said, "Walters is pulling away under steering power, Doctor. Hollis says there are likely to be gravitational side effects if the Ship generators reach full power. He says the P-ships might be sucked in and suggested that Walters move out to at least five miles so that someone would be able to tell Earth what happened to the rest of us . . ."

Listening to him, McCullough wondered if the sabotage attempt was unsuccessful, and if he wasn't killed by it and if he could get to an airlock in time, would he be able to launch himself toward Walters and the P-ships even if the alien vessel was already moving away. Angrily, he wondered why he had not simply broken away from Drew and Berryman on the way here and used a lock chamber to leave the Ship. He had thought about it but had not seriously considered doing it.

There was no shame attached to admitting that

one was a coward, he thought cynically, just as long as one did not prove it.

Inside the blister it was deathly quiet. The interference in their suit radios was so bad that they had to switch off and communicate by touching helmets. Hollis' voice came to him with a booming, indistinct quality about it, but McCullough could make it out without too much difficulty.

The physicist said, "I'm assuming that for faster-than-light travel all of the Ship's generators must be in balanced operation, and that one malfunctioning generator will cause the others to cut out and immobilize the vessel. I know enough about the power supply lines—which inside the blister are not insulated, as you can see—to blow this generator. But the result might be catastrophic for the Ship and would certainly be fatal for anyone in the immediate vicinity, which is us.

"So instead of shorting the main power supply," Hollis went on, "I propose grounding the relatively much lower control and input balancing system— those lopsided, figure-of-eight thingummies with the blue ceramic end pieces which are, I'm fairly sure, somewhat analogous to the grid of an old-fashioned radio valve. There are one of the things attached to every major piece of equipment in the blister, and I've picked out what I think are two of the most vital sections of the generator. This is what we must do . . ."

A lopsided, figure-of-eight thingummy, thought McCullough, and wondered whatever had become of the precise and rarified language of science in which Hollis was usually so bewilderingly fluent. He would pull the physicist's leg about it afterward, if there was an afterward.

They planned a simultaneous, double act of sabotage. The generators had been building up to their full operating potential for nearly twenty minutes, and there could not be very much time left to do something. The visual effects from some of the gadgetry around him were becoming quite flambuoyant. As McCullough crawled toward his assigned position, sheets of slow pink lightning curled and rippled silently all around him. His spear acquired a pale blue corona and his hair kept rising and discharging against the inside of his helmet. Every few yards magnetic eddies tugged at his weapon or the metal parts of his suit, seeking to dislodge him from the insulated catwalk and draw him into a premature act of sabotage that would certainly kill him and quite possibly wreck the whole Ship.

For reasons which were both selfish and altruistic McCullough did not want that to happen. He wanted his own skin and the Ship to suffer the minimum of damage. He realized suddenly that although he was terribly afraid for his own immediate safety he was furiously angry about the things they had done and were doing on the Ship. From the very beginning they had had no control of the situation. It had been a stupid if well intentioned muddle, and while they had changed their minds several times when new data became available, they had not really used their brains. They had been panicked into doing things, they had not allowed themselves time to think and when threatened with danger they had thought only of their own survival. All things considered, as a sampling of the species Homo so-called Sapiens, they had not made a good showing.

Suddenly McCullough was in position, looking across at Hollis who was making slow, pushing motions with one hand. The physicist was reminding him that they did not have to throw the weapons, merely launch them slowly and accurately. While he watched, Hollis held up three fingers. The silence was incredible. McCullough was holding his breath, but his pulse was thunderous and he could almost hear himself sweating. Hollis showed two fingers, one finger, then a balled fist. McCullough gently launched his spear at the target that had been assigned to him.

The weapon which had once served as part of P-Two's launcher tube was just long enough to make contact with both the figure-of-eight grid and a nearby metal bulkhead, and for the first few seconds of its travel it looked as if it would do so. But then it wobbled suddenly as one of the magnetic eddies caught it, swinging it off course. One end touched the grid and the other swung toward a fat, coppery spiral with a bright-blue halo flickering around it. McCullough gripped the catwalk tightly and managed to get his eyes closed just in time.

Even with the filtering effects of his tightly closed eyelids the flash was blinding. Every nerve in his body received a jolt that was neither pleasure, pain, pressure, heat or cold but was much worse than anything he had ever felt before in all his life. He stiffened so violently that he bounced away from the catwalk. He felt something tugging at one boot and the fear of being drawn in and electrocuted overcame his shocked paralysis. He pulled both knees up and made frantic swimming motions in an attempt to get away. But the tugging persisted. McCullough blinked furiously to dissolve the blotches covering his field of vision and saw that Hollis was gripping his boot and was towing him toward the safety of the airlock.

By the time he was through, his eyes were almost back to normal. He could see that the interior of the generator blister was again dull and lifeless. There were no chimes reverberating along the corridors and the alien voices were silent. With the interference gone, Walters was trying to contact them, saying that he had seen a flash or an explosion and were any of them alive. As soon as he had his visor open, Drew began advising him strongly to establish a base in the adjacent lock chamber with a view to discouraging any alien repair crew sent to rebuild the sabotaged generator.

But McCullough's mind was still on an earlier train of thought. Bitterly he said, "We're nothing but a bunch of stupid, well intentioned bunglers! Surely, as intelligent beings, we could have evaluated and entered a strange situation—even an alien stress situation—without making it so much worse that—that ..."

He left the sentence dangling, then went on furiously, "We *know* there are intelligent aliens on this ship—dammit, we've heard them *talking*! To them we must look like a race of juvenile delinquents or worse. We must get out, leave the Ship at once. I'll request the next supply rocket to carry spacesuits and food only. With the water supply we've discovered, this will mean that we can leave shortly after it arrives."

"And our intelligent, extraterrestrial crew, what about them?" Hollis broke in scathingly. "They haven't shown themselves up to now—at least, we're fairly sure they haven't. Why not? Are they in some kind of trouble, or are there too few of them to risk it? Are we going to leave them to do the best they can with a Two-infested, crippled Ship?"

"We aren't delinquents and we're not stupid!" Berryman said angrily. "If your e-t's are as intelligent as you say, Doctor, they will realize that everything we did came about as a result of the local situation and scientific curiosity allied to normal survival instincts! If they can't understand anything as simple as that, then they're stupid, too stupid to have built this Ship! But they did build it and so . . ."

"Kill every bloody one of them!" yelled Drew. "Wipe the buggers out!"

It was Walters who had the last word. Deafeningly, apologetically, with the volume of his transmitter turned right up he said, "*I was set up to rebroadcast your last words as the Ship carried you out of the solar system to some dire, extraterrestrial fate. This spirited exchange of ideas is being overheard by all the world.*

"I don't think the general will approve of some of the *language . . .*"

chapter sixteen

ON EARTH THERE was only one subject which, day by day and hour by hour, merited serious discussion, and that was the War on the Ship.

In this war there were no neutrals and no unaligned powers, even though the people who made up the nations and even the individual families were aligned several different ways at the same time. Everyone knew about the war, of course. There were very few who did not find it interesting, at least, while others found it so all-absorbing and exciting that they were quite willing to argue and demonstrate and burn embassy buildings over it. But the majority of people were simply worried about the safety of the men on the Ship and concerned over the many things they seemed to be doing wrong.

Everything the men said or did was, from someone's point of view, wrong.

Those scientists who thought of their specialties as being 'hard' insisted that more Ship time be devoted to gathering detailed information on structural methods and design philosophy, the operating principles and distribution of the vessel's power sources, and more, much more, data on what everyone so loosely referred to as the hyperdrive generators and the Ship's central control system. Then the scientists who were less hard—although not quite as soft as the Psychology crowd—wanted more time spent in gathering information on extraterrestrial biology and metabolism, environmental factors and e-t life-support systems. *They* wanted autopsies performed on specimens other than the Two. But it was the psychologists and their equally 'soft' relatives in sociology and anthropology who seemed to be the least demanding and at the same time the most positive in their recommendations.

For the psychologists were having a long succession of field days. Not only were minor and major Ship incidents studied and evaluated and discussed at great lenth, every single recorded word and inflection was subjected to a most rigorous analysis. So much so that on one occasion a short, odd-sounding laugh from Walters threw one group of space medics into a near-panic for three days until they discovered that the high, uneven pitch of the pilot's voice, so suggestive of hysteria and imminent crack-up, was due to natural distortion in the incoming signal.

Despite the dropping of an occasional brick, the psychologist's picture of conditions on the Ship, the interaction of the characters involved, the general emotional and moral climate and the unique environmental pressures to which the men were being subjected, was reasonably complete and accurate and their recommendations sound.

At least, the psychologists considered them so . . .

The majority of these psychological discussions were broadcast on radio and TV, of course, as was practically everything pertaining to the Ship. But there was one group whose recommendations, by their very nature, could not be made public—even, and especially, if their recommendations were to be adopted.

This group suggested that since the emotional situation arising out of the environmental conditions on the Ship was known in broad outline and the psychological makeup of the men currently inhabiting it was available in great detail, it should be possible to devise certain stimuli which would return a large measure of control to the Prometheus authorities instead of allowing it to remain in the hands and ethically confused minds of men who were too close to their problem to have a balanced appreciation of it. They insisted that the problem was basically one of psychological maladjustment and was solely their responsibility, and as they were the people who would have to solve it they did not think it fair that they should have this responsibility without also being given a measure of control over the situation.

They also mentioned the fact that the position of the sun with respect to Earth and the P-ships would very shortly make direct communication impossible. Outgoing messages, which hitherto had been receivable only by the P-ships, as well as incoming signals, would have to be relayed through the Russian circum-Venus station. The Russians were being very generous with their facilities, but they would know every word that passed in each direction and would undoubtedly use the information gained to their own advantage to complicate an already overcomplicated political situation. For this reason alone a decision on their recommendations should be taken as soon as possible.

For the less emotionally mature, the Ship had replaced all the variations of Cowboys and Indians. Day after day all over the world, Walters had his suit slashed by the first Two, Colonel Morrison met his grisly death, and McCullough, who was a difficult and unsatisfactory character for children to portray, moved around doing nothing, apparently, but change his mind.

Between the children and the eggheads lay the tremendous multitude who were only moderately adult and whose intelligence was average. These were the people who listened avidly to what they referred to as the War News and who greedily absorbed every fact and speculation that came from the more informed commentators on the radio and TV, even though many of them must have been aware that the commentators could not possibly be more informed than their listeners.

They watched closely while the latest photographs and sketches—tidied up and dramatized a little for TV presentation—were discussed by panels of scientists from every field of knowledge and every degree of eminence. They listened to so many analyses, theories, and predictions, they were exposed to so many different opinions and viewpoints and ethical yardsticks in so short a space of time that they were forced either to choose sides, or to make up their own minds as to what was right or wrong or politically expedient.

Some of them reacted by breaking windows and overturning cars, or agitated for the Twos to be brought under the protection of the UN or the USPCA, or started funds for sending comforts for the troops, well aware of the utterly fantastic cost of sending even an ounce of comfort to those fifty-million-mile-distant warriors. But there were others, not a great number to begin with, who went through the intensely uncomfortable business of thinking for themselves until the realization came that their world had changed, that it was no longer *the* world but just *a* world with all that that implied.

This small but rapidly growing faction was only one of the many pressure groups who felt they had a say in the control of Prometheus.

The original idea in making every phase of the project open to the public had been to arouse interest in space flight generally and to gain the support of the voters for the enormous cost of the hardware —in short, a large-scale P.R. job. It was a noble project which had, unfortunately, to be paid for by people who were not all noble. But now Prometheus had gone sour, its Ship-side personnel seemed to be devolving into vicious and sadistic killers while back at home nobility was breaking out in some of the most unlikely places.

On Earth as well as on the Ship, Prometheus was getting out of control . . .

"*. . . While you were hunting for Ship water and hamstringing that generator,*" General Brady's voice rattled at them, "*you had to be rough on the aliens and their equipment. We aren't entirely blaming you for this, but we think you are exercising far too much initiative. Public opinion is hardening against you and against Prometheus as a whole, even though the majority are still being thrilled by the 'war' and the exploits of their scientist heroes. But this is a temporary, unstable, even sick reaction. There is a steadily growing body of opinion which is openly* *critical of your behavior. It accuses you, and through you us, of behaving like barbarians! It insists that you are doing little more than looting the Ship of its scientific booty.*

"This has got to stop!"

A radio from one of the damaged suits floated near the outer wall of the lock chamber, attached to the plating by its antenna lead. The natural distortion caused by the helmet 'phones being overloaded so as to act as loudspeakers was increased by the anger in General Brady's voice, which carried clearly over fifty million miles.

". . . We have begun the countdown for a multiple launch—three high-acceleration vehicles containing food and extra spacesuits only. Until they arrive seven weeks from now you will sit tight and do nothing! Your only activity will be collecting and storing Ship water for the return trip.

"Establish a base in one of the lock chambers close to the P-ships and defend it if necessary, but not by taking the offensive! Try using your ingenuity to avoid killing Twos now, and do not molest them or injure them in any way even if they begin repairing the generator! Quite a few of us here are far from convinced that the Two life-form is in fact the nonintelligent animal you say it is. Exploration of the Ship will cease forthwith and you will cease trying to experiment with its power and control systems. Neither will you endanger yourselves, and quite possibly the future of our society, by attempting to communicate with the intelligent aliens who may be on the Ship . . ."

Berryman reached out quickly and turned the volume down to a whisper. He looked from McCullough to Drew and Hollis and then back again. His smile was all too plainly forced as he said, "Considering all that the general has just said, the action we are contemplating is tantamount to mutiny."

Hollis said, "I agree." They both looked and sounded frightened, as if they were already having second thoughts.

"He doesn't know what he's talking about," said Drew angrily. "Either that or he doesn't believe what we've told him!"

And there is a really uncomfortable idea, thought McCullough, then went on quickly, "These orders are harsh, inflexible and ill-considered. In a short time they will, like the earlier ones, be amended and qualified. We'll still be forbidden to kill Twos—unless circumstances make it absolutely necessary. Exploration will be allowed—within certain limits which will not be clearly defined. It will be suggested that we obtain further data on the hyperdrive generators—if this can be done without upsetting the aliens, or without running *too* great a risk of upsetting the aliens. Gradually the orders will contain so many qualifiers we will be back in square one, but with our self-confidence reduced and our tempers drastically shortened."

Cynically, McCullough went on, "Instead of being heroes it seems we are to become scapegoats—at least, that is the way it looks to me. But this means that we will have to be allowed some freedom of action, otherwise they would not be able to blame us for everything that is happening . . ."

"In other words," said Drew grimly, "if we can't please anyone we can at least try to please ourselves."

Hollis said doubtfully, "He wasn't at all sympathetic about our troubles, and it is only three days since the colonel died and he didn't mention him at all. But suggesting that we will be held responsible for everything is going too far, don't you think?"

"Perhaps," said McCullough. "But you agree that if *we* are too close to the problem, *they* are much too far away?"

The three men nodded in turn and suddenly Berryman laughed. He said, "This must be the first mutiny in history where the captain is the ringleader . . ."

He broke off as the quality of the whisper coming from the 'phones altered, and at McCullough's nod he turned up the volume again.

"*. . . And he has no real appreciation of the harm his anger and hostility toward you can cause,*" said a low, sympathetic, female voice. It went on, "*In terms of physical distance alone you must feel cut off, separated, even rejected by your friends and perhaps even your race. In a very real sense you have withdrawn from reality, you have lost touch with the world and life as it should be lived. The psychic disturbances, the emotional dislocations, the constant and cumulative frustration of even the simplest natural urges—even the act of eating and drinking is artificial and unnatural where you are concerned—is more than enough without adding the terrible responsibility of First Contact.*

"*I don't mean to suggest that any of you have reached the point of major instability,*" she went on warmly, "*or that you are not quite sane. I do suggest, however, that your judgment and reactions are seriously affected by your present situation and may no longer be entirely trustworthy. This is what is bothering the general, too, because he is being held responsible for everything that you people think or do, and every minority group in the world is trying to pressure him into taking fifty mutually exclusive courses of action! We all admit he's a genius where astronautics hardware and logistics are concerned, but let's face it, fellows, he is no psychologist . . ."*

McCullough switched off the radio feeling angry and a little frightened. What idiot had been responsible for turning a woman psychologist loose on the Prometheus Control transmitter? Previously there had been no mention whatsoever of the mental effects of separation in time and space from the world of normal existence. When such effects had become manifest they had been ignored—the P-ship personnel had been treated as if they were on an extended EVA and their distance was five hundred miles from home rather than fifty million.

Emotionally they had been made to feel very close to home. Continuous radio contact plus the knowledge that practically everyone in the world was sharing their experiences and feeling concern for them were just two of the factors aimed at achieving this, and there were probably others which only the space medics knew about. But whoever had allowed a psychologist ignorant of these factors, especially such a disturbingly female one as this, to talk to them and cause them to question their own sanity was either stupid or criminally irresponsible.

"Walters is listening," said McCullough. "He can tell us if she says anything really important. Right now I'd like you to listen to this tape again. I have another theory."

For several minutes the sounds of their dash from the Twos' enclosure to the generator blister filled the lock chamber. McCullough asked them to pay particular attention to the two alien voices. When the playback was complete he said, "In my opinion the first voice is a recording transmitted in conjunction with the warning chimes—each group of word-sounds is identical in tone, volume and length of transmission. The second voice is none of these things. Its overall tone is different, volume and inflection vary enormously and the message transmitted by the first voice is repeated, after a fashion, by the second. Perhaps I should say that the message is not so much repeated as parodied by the second voice.

"I feel that certain words are repeated too often for it to be an intelligent communication. It is as if one word in a sentence was repeated twenty times and sung in different keys. Many of the sounds seem to be sheer organic noise and sense-free—you have heard them.

"My new theory," McCullough went on, looking at the three men in turn, "is supported by all the facts. Briefly it is that the alien crew have no effective control of their vessel, that its operation is almost entirely automatic and that the experimental animals have overrun the ship. The second alien voice belongs to one of the crew, or perhaps a descendant of the original crew, and it is an intelligent being. However, it is not at present a rational being, or even sane . . ."

While he had been talking, McCullough found that his finger had instinctively gone to the suit radio switch. There was some vague idea in his mind of putting in a full report to Control and shifting responsibility by calling Earth for a Second Opinion. But Brady's opinions would not be helpful, McCullough knew from short and bitter experience, and he himself had insisted many times that the people on the Ship were better informed on all aspects of the situation and should therefore make their own decisions. He could have Walters send a full report, or even a slightly edited report, later.

Firmly McCullough took his hand and mind off the radio.

chapter seventeen

JOINED BY THEIR command module airlocks the two P-ships were positioned a few yards above the generator blister so that Walters would be able to detect any attempt to repair the human-inflicted damage. The arrival of an alien repair crew was not considered likely, but the presence of Walters on watch meant that everyone else could be gainfully employed inside the Ship on what McCullough referred to as wide-angle cultural contact and Drew, with more honesty, called an offensive patrol.

Their real purpose, no matter what they chose to call it or how much double-thinking they did around it, was to kill Twos. They would also hunt down and exterminate any other alien life-form which might prove dangerous to the intelligent extraterrestrials on the Ship or themselves.

"Thanks to the Doctor we know all their vital spots," Drew said as they were preparing to leave their hull lock chamber, "and provided we keep cool and pause for the necessary instant to take proper aim, killing the beasts will be relatively easy. But we should not take on more than one of them at a time unless we have the advantage of a solid defensive position. This isn't very sporting since there are four of us, but we cannot afford casualties."

McCullough was listening to Drew but thinking about Walters. One did not have to be a psychologist to know that the pilot was close to the breaking point. Even though he was in the least physical danger of all, Walters was in one respect absorbing more punishment than any of them. Prometheus Control, General Brady and assorted space medical people were continually hammering at him, he being the only member of the expedition they could talk to with any chance of getting an immediate reply. And because he was the only one available, Brady was being much tougher on Walters than the situation really warranted. The general was trying to get through to McCullough and the others, but all the anger and recriminations and outright threats sounded as if they were being directed at Walters alone.

McCullough no longer communicated direct with the general—he was usually too busy in the Ship and Walters was in a position to pass on any new or constructive suggestions if there were any. This was, he knew, very unfair to the pilot since he frequently had to wait days for the chance to do so, days during which he could never be sure whether the other men in the ship were alive or dead. When, at the conclusion of a particularly bad session with Brady, one of the cosmonauts on the circum-Venus station which was now relaying all transmissions added a few words wishing him luck, Walters' reaction was both revealing and quite unexpected in a grown man.

The pilot needed company. McCullough or Hollis,

the only two who had operational spacesuits, should have visited him more often. But somehow there was never time. Something was always happening in the Ship . . .

The doctor became aware suddenly that the lock entrance was open and Drew was beside it, saying ". . . And remember, this is not a game. If anyone feels like treating it as one they should remind themselves that the nearest hospital is sixty million miles away and the ambulance service is bad . . ."

On the way to the animal enclosure, they encountered—singly—three of the tentacled aliens and killed them. Since it was now generally accepted that the Twos were nonintelligent lab animals the job had been performed with efficiency and, McCullough noted, quite a lot of enthusiasm. Drew had noticed it, too, and he kept repeating his warnings about thinking of the operation as a game until they reached the cages, and would probably have continued if McCullough had not cut him short.

"I agree with Drew," he said firmly. "We must be entirely cold-blooded about this. But before we put our plan into effect I would like to gain a better idea of their physical capabilities. To begin with, how did they break out?"

It was between mealtimes for the e-t's so they had a chance to search the area thoroughly.

The animals' quarters occupied a cylindrical volume of space roughly eighty yards in length and twenty in diameter. It was divided into pens of various sizes by heavy wire mesh stretched between a framework of tubing, so that the caged animals were always in sight of anyone in the four personnel corridors which ran fore and aft along the sides of the enclosure. The food and water dispensers also differed in size and complexity, and were fitted to the common wall between two cages so as to serve both. Some of the cages were still occupied, by drifting, dessicated carcasses whose edible parts were missing.

From the condition of the bodies, the damage to large areas of the restraining mesh and the condition of the food dispensers, they were able to obtain a fairly good idea of what had happened.

One or more of the dispensers had failed. Whether the failure was due to a design fault or the rough eating habits of the animals concerned was impossible to say. But the result was an attack on the wire mesh, a successful attack in most cases, which had forced an opening into the operating dispensers in adjacent cages or into enclosures containing smaller edible life-forms. The transfer of animals between cages had so increased the demand on the remaining dispensers that they, too, had broken down until only a few machines were still operating. An attempt had been made to control the mass breakout by electrification of sections of the wire mesh, but this had been a hasty, jury-rigged installation which had also broken down in several places.

Judging by the condition of the bodies, the majority of the other animals had been unable to defend themselves against the terrible horn and tentacles of the Twos, although a small number must have escaped through gaps torn in the mesh, otherwise there would have been only one species infesting the Ship. But there was one large, caterpillar-like animal who had never had a chance. All McCullough could tell from its remains was that it had no skeleton to speak of, its body being surrounded by great bands of muscle, and its head section, which was heavily boned, contained four manipulators or feelers of some kind in addition to the usual sensory equipment. Its hide was pale gray and very smooth, like that of a walrus.

In a nearby enclosure, however, the Twos had met something which even they could not stand against. For a long time McCullough and the others stared at the drifting Two carcasses, stripped of all edible tissue so that little more than the bony carapace remained, and at the cluster of tiny holes punched through the half-inch-thick shell.

It was Berryman who spoke first.

"And now," he said gravely, "we are looking for an emotionally disturbed alien with a machine gun . . ."

But they all had far too much to do before the Twos began arriving for lunch to give this new development the discussion it deserved.

The first step was to disconnect the wiring from the electrified sections of mesh—it would not be a good thing to be accidentally electrocuted while doing battle with the Twos. Then from the small or more damaged food dispensers they stripped lengths of cable and metal piping and threaded these into the torn sections of mesh, repairing and reinforcing their cage's sides and barring its severely warped doors. They did not make any provision for evacuation if their plan went wrong, although it was obvious that they were all thinking about it while they worked and talked loudly about the probable effects of shutting off the Ship's animals from what must be the only source of food and water.

All the other dispensers had been wrecked, accidentally by the Twos or deliberately by the men.

"Poisoning them would be safer," said Berryman when their cage had been made as secure as possible, "if we knew what was toxic to them and if we had some of it . . ."

"Too slow," said McCullough.

"Six inches of cold aluminum alloy," said Drew, "is toxic to everything."

"Company," said Hollis.

Three of the tentacled e-t's and a pair of the white-furred flying carpets had arrived and were heading toward their cage. It became a civil war almost at once.

As soon as the furry Type Three came within striking distance, a Two lashed out with its tentacle, the bony tip ripping a six-inch gash in the white fur. While the Three flapped helplessly in the center of the corridor, the Two steadied itself against the mesh and launched a second and more deadly attack, this time crisscrossing the pelt with deep and visibly widening channels which oozed bright red. The Three began to undulate rapidly until it was fluttering like a thick, bloody flag in a high wind. Then suddenly it was just a tattered, lifeless rag and its attacker, a very messy eater, began to feed.

Meanwhile the second Two was not having things all its own way. Somehow the furry animal had managed both to evade its attacker's tentacles and to attach itself to the Two's unprotected back where those four deadly weapons could not be brought to bear. At first McCullough thought he was seeing the e-t version of the old adage about holding a tiger by the tail, but then he saw that the furry body of the Three was squeezing down and between the roots of the threshing tentacles where the Two's eyes were situated, blinding it, and then extending further onto and across the underbelly until it blocked the breathing apertures.

When the Two was dead, the furry animal did not try to eat it, but instead undulated over to the mesh. Possibly it was a vegetarian.

During the fight the unoccupied Two had attacked the mesh, probing and worrying and slapping at it with horn and tentacles, then bouncing back to the corridor wall net to hurl itself carapace first like a living cannonball against the wire. McCullough had wondered how the animals had been able to break out of their cages in the first place, since the security arrangements had seemed adequate for such a relatively small life-form, but as the mesh twanged and bulged inward under the onslaught of this single, angry specimen, he was no longer puzzled. Finally the Two, tired of beating its head against the mesh, insinuated a couple of feet of one of its tentacles in an attempt to pull the wire apart.

Immediately Drew gripped the tentacle, planted both feet firmly against the mesh and pulled the Two hard against the wire while the spear in his other hand drove forward in a single, twisting, lethal stab. The beast's tentacles threshed briefly and were still, then there was another Two charging the mesh, and another.

The dispenser began making soft, chuffing sounds. It emitted a slow, untidy jet of water and a series of gray round objects of the size and shape of a large orange from a spigot which had had its teat chewed off. The round objects had the consistency of porridge, Berryman reported when one of them hit the side of his head, and added that the smell and taste—it had splattered forward onto his nose and lips—were not entirely unpleasant.

They became too busy to talk shortly after that;

the job of killing Twos was not as easy as Drew had made it appear.

They were badly hampered by weightlessness, which forced them either to hold onto a Two or to twist their feet through the mesh to use their spears effectively. But very often the Twos presented far too many tentacles, and anchoring themselves by twisting a foot into the mesh was asking to have it smashed by the hard tip of a tentacle or impaled on a horn. Without some form of support their aim suffered and most of the force behind their thrusts was expended on getting through the mesh, so that what little remained was enough only to push the Twos away and inflict superficial injuries if any. The reaction from such a lunge sent the men spinning helplessly so that they were in as much danger from the spears of their friends as the horns of the Twos.

"This is a stupid plan," gasped McCullough as he knocked away a spear which was coming at his face.

"Since it was your plan," said Berryman from the other side of the cage, "I must decline to comment."

"Hold still, everyone," said Drew. "I want to try something . . ."

During the few minutes' pause while he explained and demonstrated his idea, the mesh, particularly the places which had been patched and reinforced, took a savage beating. Reinforcing cable stretched and snapped, lengths of piping buckled and began slipping out of position, and it would be only a matter of time before the Twos were inside the cage with them.

Following Drew's instructions, they launched themselves like ungainly swordfish from the panel of the dispenser, arms extended stiffly before them and hands gripping their weapons. They jumped in unison so as to minimize the danger of spearing each other, the idea being to aim themselves in the general direction of their target and at the last moment guide the tip of their spears through the mesh. The creatures possessed enough weight and inertia not to be pushed away before a deep wound was inflicted and, since the combined length of arms and spear was much greater than that of the e-t's horn or tentacles there would be little danger of retaliation.

It worked.

After the first few abortive attempts it became a drill. They each chose a target, kicked themselves away from the food dispenser cabinet, and the three targets died. But there were always more to take their places, squeezing tentacles through the wire, jabbing with that long, obscene horn and gobbling like frantic turkeys. For McCullough it became a continuing nightmare of killing the same Two over and over again. He had lost count of the times they had launched themselves from the dispenser, now slippery with a scummy mixture of food, water and e-t blood, to dive through air that was like a thick soup of the same recipe, to kill that Two once again.

A number of the white-furred Threes had squeezed between the Twos and were clinging to the wire and absorbing—McCullough could not see exactly how—the streamers and gobbets of water and food drifting toward them. There were even two of them inside the cage, having wriggled through a loosened patch, flapping and undulating through the air like great furry sting-rays. All the men had been careful not to kill the type Three aliens—after seeing how one of them had dealt with a Two they considered them allies rather than enemies. In addition, not killing them introduced a certain amount of discrimination into the exercise so that they could think of it as being something less than a brutal, bloody massacre.

McCullough tried to think of other things while the slaughter proceeded.

Between mealtimes the animal enclosure had been surprisingly clean, so that the dispenser cabinet must also fulfill the duty of a waste-disposal unit. But while the waste water and food would no doubt be reprocessed, the material which could not be reclaimed would be pumped to the outer hull and disposed of, which meant that the plumbing associated with the waste-disposal system would be metal piping which, because it did not have to carry an electrical current, would not have to be insulated at any point between the dispenser and the hull outlet. As soon as this was all over they would be able to hook onto it with their suit antennae and contact Walters.

He felt rather pleased with himself for being able to reason things out like this while engaged in the not quite routine job of killing Twos. Then suddenly there were no more targets. The still-living Twos were retreating along the corridors, dragging the bodies of their dead friends with them when they could so that they would not go hungry, and the dispenser, which had ceased producing half an hour since, went dramatically into reverse.

Heavy protective panels slid aside to reveal large openings covered with safety grills. Drifting food, water and other debris moved toward the openings, picking up speed as they went. So great was the force of suction that the air made a high-pitched whistle as it went through the grill and within a few minutes the cage was clear. But there was more to come. From the eight corners of the enclosure a thin, foaming, sharp-smelling liquid spurted out, immediately followed by eight high-pressure sprays of water. By the time the dispenser had shut itself off, the men and the two furry Threes inside the cage were like the air, clean, fresh and slightly damp.

Outside the cage dead Twos drifted and spun slowly, stiff-tentacled, like fossilized starfish. Above, below and all around them the mesh was thick with them, as if it was some kind of alien flypaper which had not been changed for too long a time.

Berryman linked his antenna to the dispenser plumbing and made contact with Walters. He tried to speak but obviously could not get a word in edgeways. Watching, McCullough saw him close his eyes tightly as if there was something he did not want to see, something much worse than the ghastly spectacle all around them. Finally he spoke.

"We're in trouble," he said dully. "Walters is— upset. Brady has been working on him again, and that girl. She sounds a nice girl, he says, but she confuses him. The first supply rocket is off course. She didn't actually tell him that we were bad boys and if we didn't start doing as we were told again the other two might miss as well. It was just that public opinion was touchy and it was difficult to make promises when the men at the Ship kept messing things up. He says she mentioned some very personal stuff, material he never expected to hear mentioned, privileged information. He's thinking of all the people who have heard everything she said—the men on the Venus station and all their people in Russia. Everybody will soon know. He's very unhappy about it."

Berryman stopped and took a deep breath. Fatigue

and tension made it into a tremendous, ludicrous yawn, but nobody laughed. He went on, "So he blabbed everything to Brady. Your new theory, our plans, everything. He says he couldn't help it. He says he wants to be a *good* boy again so's they'll let him go home . . ."

chapter eighteen

FOR THREE DAYS they barricaded themselves inside the dispenser cage during mealtimes and killed Twos. As expected, the number of e-t casualties diminished sharply each day. This was, of course, due to the fact of there being ample food available outside the cage in the form of previously slain animals. On the fourth day they tried a different approach.

A series of food caches were built up in compartments opening off the corridors leading from the enclosure to one of the hull airlocks. By this time they had discovered how to turn off the food dispensers at will and they had towed the dead e-t's to the nearest lock and dumped them into space, so that the Twos which remained in the Ship were becoming very hungry.

The operation of placing a trail of food between the enclosure and the lock chamber, during the few minutes before mealtimes when it would have its maximum effect, was a dangerous one but well worth

164

the risks. The end result was a lock chamber crowded with Twos fighting over a small food cache so fiercely that they were usually oblivious of the fact that they had suddenly been sealed in and that Hollis or McCullough were outside the hull, opening the compartment to space.

They bagged as many as six Twos at a time that way.

On the ninth day McCullough decided that their original purpose of drastically reducing the numbers of Twos roaming the Ship had been accomplished and they could all return to more constructive forms of activity.

The decision on what to do about Walters was not so easily taken, but McCullough could not put off making it any longer.

Punishment or retribution of any kind was ruled out, of course, since that would involve varying degrees of criticism or rejection by his friends. Alone as he had been on the P-ship for weeks on end the pilot was particularly sensitive to this form of punishment, and he had already soaked up more than enough of it from General Brady. Dirty fighting and psychological warfare, so far as McCullough was concerned, were becoming synonymous.

"I should have come to see you sooner," he told Walters as he opened his visor after passing through the inner seal. He waved vaguely toward the port and the frigid, decompressed Twos drifting outside and added, "We were very busy."

"Yes," said the pilot, smiling. "I took some very good pictures of the spring-cleaning . . ."

Walters' voice was quiet and pleasant, his features relaxed and his hands and fingers yellow and bloodless, so tightly was he gripping the sides of his couch.

Awkwardly, McCullough said, "I won't say that we don't blame you, not again. Telling the truth too often can make it sound like a lie. And, well, don't worry if it happens to you again. You are aware of what they are trying to do to you so it won't be so easy for them next time, and they might even change their approach."

"They have," said Walters. "Just before you arrived, that girl told me they would not divert the other supply rockets no matter what fool stunt we pulled or how much trouble we caused them. Obviously this news is supposed to make us all break down and weep out of sheer gratitude that mamma still loves us even when we've been naughty.

"I wish I hadn't read so many psychology books," he ended bitterly. "It has made me cynical."

McCullough laughed. He said, "Cynicism is a very good defense. Throw in a little sympathy for the enemy—Brady, that is, not the Twos—while a good, hefty shot of megalomania might help as well. You start by doubting everything they tell you and questioning all their motives, at the same time trying to appreciate the general's position, but not to the extent that you fail to realize the true importance of the part we have to play in all this. So you doubt Brady, you feel sorry for him and, in your quiet, respectful fashion, you also feel superior to him. Get the idea?"

"Of late," said Walters doubtfully, "I have become much less quiet and respectful."

"That is because you haven't been feeling superior enough," said McCullough drily. He went on, "We are the experts in this particular situation. It is ridiculous to expect us to obey people who know less about it than we do—people who, if they were to regain complete control over us, are under so much pressure from so many different directions that they are incapable of giving proper orders anyway."

McCullough waited then, without appearing to wait, wondering if the pilot would seize the bait or even if he was aware of it. He was and he did.

"You mentioned them regaining complete control over us," said Walters quickly. "Other than the control, which is as you know far from complete, imposed by service discipline and the habit of obedience, how can they influence us?"

"This is rather awkward for me," said McCullough, preparing to slide imperceptibly from questionable, rule-of-thumb psychology into outright fiction, "because I didn't want to talk about this until I was surer of my facts. But it seems to me that we may have been the subjects of a form of conditioning which was designed to support and guide us as well as furnishing Prometheus with a large measure of control. By this I mean that it was subtle enough not to interfere with mentation and at the same time leave us unaware that we were being helped and controlled. How exactly this conditioning was implanted I don't know, although I suspect that the hours we spent listening to canned lectures in the simulator may have had something to do with it. But the method used to reinforce the conditioning and at the same time control us is, I'm fairly sure, the radio transmissions from the Cape.

"The mechanics of the process," McCullough went on seriously, "might involve the use of certain key words and phrases but would, I'm pretty sure, be more likely to depend on the tonal quality of voice used—they could heterodyne their AF with sub- or ultra-sonics to obtain a kind of subliminal effect on the audio frequency. But for various reasons the conditioning broke down or was considerably weakened and they lost a large measure of their control over us."

Natural radio interference with the signal could have been one factor, McCullough went on to explain, and the constant relaying of transmissions through the suit radios had probably attenuated the effect even more. It was not surprising, therefore, that the men who had Control's orders relayed to them from the P-ship had been able to exercise discretion in the matter of obeying orders, while Walters, who was in direct radio contact, had never had a chance of resisting them.

"That makes me feel much better," said the pilot when McCullough had finished talking. "It even gives me an excuse for future misdemeanors, if any. But surely Brady's psychological weapon is two-edged. It caused to be made public information which he would have preferred to remain secret; namely, the extermination—massacre, he calls it—of the Twos. Rather than risk the chance of the listening world hearing something even more unpleasant, he might leave me alone."

"I doubt it," said McCullough.

"But if he goes on," said Walters angrily, "it means he is pushing a psychological abort button! He will be softening us up until, instead of being able to think and carry out complex technical activities, we'll be just so many jellies unable to think or act at all, much less obey orders. Is he trying to wreck the Project? Isn't it also possible that he could push a button and ignite our return fuel supply? Was provision made for this in case the e-t's turned out to be baddies and threatened the security of the world?

"All of a sudden I don't trust Brady, and I dislike being treated like part of the hardware."

He broke off as he became aware of McCullough's expression, then said quickly, "I don't really believe any of that, but there is an easy way to deal with the possibility. Next time we're in contact I'll tell the listening world that if there is an unexplained explosion out here it will have been caused by Brady." He laughed suddenly. "But your real danger is me! With this information and all the spare time at my disposal I might analyze and reproduce this conditioning effect. *My* word would be law then, and I could wrap you all around my little finger!"

"As I said," McCullough smiled as he turned to go, "a *little* megalomania is a good thing . . ."

On the way back to the Ship, McCullough found himself questioning some of his own motives. He had been telling lies to the pilot, suggesting that Walters had not been really responsible for his apparent treachery, by blaming everything on a form of conditioning which might not even be workable; and not solely as an act of kindness. McCullough himself needed support and reassurance. He wanted as many people on his side as possible, which meant that he could not risk Walters going over to Brady. If the pilot sided actively with Control instead of the men in the Ship, McCullough could not bear to think of the consequences. In the frighteningly simple world of emotional relationships and physical survival, Walters' friendship could be assured only if he was to become completely and utterly hostile to the general.

And so McCullough himself was guilty of pressing psychological push buttons and treating a human being as part of the hardware. Worse, he was pressing them without fully understanding what he was doing or what the end result might be. Worst of all was the fact that what he was doing did not trouble McCullough's conscience as much or as often as it should.

His conscience seemed to be developing thick and widespread calluses. He wondered how long it would be before he became completely decivilized.

Progress within the Ship during the next few days was erratic. Berryman came out in a livid, itching rash which lasted for one whole day and caused McCullough to have horrible visions of everyone going down with the e-t equivalent of bubonic plague carried by dead Twos, before it faded completely. It was only then that Hollis, Drew and Berryman admitted smugly to eating a few ounces of alien porridge every day for the past week. McCullough warned them of the possibility of dangerous long-term cumulative effects—the fact that Berryman's allergy symptoms had cleared up in so short a time did not necessarily mean that the food was completely nontoxic. But then McCullough realized that he was beginning to sound like General Brady and that the three men were expecting compliments instead of criticism, so he added gravely that the cumulative effect of the toxins would probably take the form of a long, wasting, ultimately fatal disease indistinguishable from old age.

Spurred on by this act of moral cowardice they immediately announced plans for domesticating the Threes . . .

They did it by first using the porridge to gain their

trust, by punishment to teach them not to wrap their furry bodies around a human being's head—although there was no real danger here as they could be peeled off easily with human fingers, and the punishment was very light—and by petting, particularly when it took the form of combing their fur with stiffened fingers. Several of the Threes became attached, literally, to Berryman and Drew, and Hollis and McCullough began picking out Threes and trying to make friends with them.

Their fur was pleasant to touch and they seemed very friendly and demonstrative—just like dogs, in fact. McCullough suspected that, like dogs, the scratching gave them pleasure because it helped dislodge parasites and he began to wonder about the habits of alien fleas. Also like dogs they were useful as well as friendly—they could sense Twos at a distance and this early warning system saved lives many times over.

Despite the three successful operations in the enclosure and the subsequent strategy which had lured a large number of the beasts into lock chambers and the vacuum of space, their movements within the Ship were still being badly hampered by Twos.

Mean, vicious and very hungry Twos.

By following the supply ducting back from the food dispensers they had found the compartment—whose doors, fortunately, had remained Two-proof—where the food was processed for distribution to the various cages. Their first act had been to shut off the food supply—which had been accomplished with very little damage to processing equipment—with the idea of forcing the remaining Twos to kill each other off for food. But this had turned out to be a very slow business and, while they occasionally came on an animal which had been killed and eaten by its own species, there were indications that the surviving Twos—their numbers were estimated at not over twenty—preferred human beings as food.

The investigation was proceeding, McCullough told himself, but an unbiased, hypothetical observer would have said that the humans were being hunted all over the Ship.

chapter nineteen

THEY INVESTIGATED, OR were forced to take cover near, the area of the Power Room. This was the compartment in which all the heavy power cables for the generators and the Ship lighting supplies had their origin, and they spent two days in the area without being able to find a way in. So far as they could see, the compartment was heavily shielded and sealed tightly against all intruders, including members of the Ship's crew.

As the work of charting the vessel's interior continued, other blank areas appeared, compartments which were completely sealed off against everyone and everything.

"Like it says in my car instruction booklet," said Hollis, trying manfully to hide his disappointment, "repair or maintenance should be handled only by a qualified mechanic or service station . . ."

One of the compartments which they entered easily contained large quantities of food and liquids other than water in what was obviously weightless packaging. This time it was the Threes rather than the men who acted, quite happily, as guinea pigs— McCullough wanted to dispel a lingering doubt which was troubling him that the containers might hold paint instead of soup. But it was the labeling system used to identify the containers which caused most of the discussion.

It was Hollis who tried finally to sum up.

"We agree that the line of characters overprinted on the label is some kind of service routing and identification code or serial number. We think it is a number rather than a word because of the repetition of certain characters and because similar combinations were found on Ship subassemblies and structural details. Markings incorporated in the label itself, which are similar to those found near airlock controls and service panels, are words identifying its contents with possibly the addition of some purely advertising material. The pictorial content of some of the labels is confusing, but then an illustration of a slice of bacon would not give an alien very much information about a pig. We must assume that the containers hold some kind of edible animal or vegetable tissue, although there is a faint possibility that . . ."

"The labels," Berryman said, grinning, "may carry a picture of the chef."

Hollis ignored him and continued, "The fact that the whole compartment is below-average Ship temperature, and that many of the storage cabinets are additionally refrigerated, supports the food theory. But the part which puzzles me is the picture of the Three on the door of that big refrigerated cabinet, and the tools or eating utensils and assorted collection of small packages inside it which also carry pictures of a Three. Is the Three, or certain parts of it, perhaps, some kind of delicacy?"

Drew shook his head. He said, "In our house we didn't keep the caviar in the cutlery drawer."

McCullough had been thinking hard while the physicist had been talking. He said suddenly, "The delicacies are too small, some of them, and too carefully wrapped to be food, I think, and the utensils are very sharp and their packaging also bears the emblem of a somewhat stylized Three. To me this suggests—well, what animal do you associate with medicine and errands of mercy?"

Hollis said, "A red—but no, that isn't an animal. A snake! The staff and coiled serpents of Asclepius. Or—or do you mean a St. Bernard?"

McCullough nodded and Berryman began stroking the Three which was wrapped around his hips and thighs like a great furry diaper.

"Nice doggie," he said happily.

But the great majority of the compartments they examined were puzzling without being informative. They were large compartments containing eight, twelve and sometimes sixteen big, hollow cylinders of some kind of plastic material supported along the center of the room by taut but flexible cables. The cylinders were just over three yards in length and were encircled at intervals of a foot or so by wide, flexible bands of rubbery materials which compressed the soft, hollow tube and made it look a little like a caterpillar. The material of the cylinder was thickly padded on the inside.

The compartments were fitted with lighting fixtures, cabinets, and various enigmatic items whose general design and coloring were less utilitarian than anything previously met with in the Ship. Invariably, one of the cabinets bore the picture of a stylized Three on its door and in some of them the contents showed signs of having been used. In some of the compartments there were pictures on the walls— large, fuzzy pictures which seemed to show trees growing horizontally with branches doubling as extra roots, or things which looked like heaps of varicolored spaghetti, or illustrations, sometimes covering most of the wall, of something resembling marble or coarse-grained wood.

Sometimes a thorough search of these compartments brought to light mislaid or discarded books, diagrams and photographs. Some of the books were illustrated, the diagrams were purely technical, and the photographs were even more confusing since they pictured things or people or events which were completely alien.

"I wish," said Hollis bitterly as he turned one of the photographs, playing cards or beer mats over and over in a vain attempt to find a viewpoint which made sense, "that they had been a little more untidy. You can find out an awful lot about a person from the contents of his wastepaper basket."

"If these cylinders are some kind of tubular hammock," said Berryman to McCullough, "and I don't see what else they can be, the only e-t they will fit is that big caterpillar we found half eaten in the animal enclosure. But what really bothers me is the number of these dormitory compartments and the number of hammocks in each one. What *was* this Ship? A troop transport? Some kind of colonization project which went wrong?"

"Maybe a big ship needs a crew to match," Drew put in quickly. "But where the blazes are they?"

McCullough shook his head. He said, "My theory

is that it was, and is, a very small crew. If there had been a large number of them when the Twos broke out, we would have found traces of them—carcasses, bones, inedible remnants. How that particular caterpillar happened to be in that cage I don't know, but . . ."

"Suppose it wasn't intelligent," Hollis broke in, "but a species physically resembling the intelligent e-t life-form. Before we sent a man into space we tested apes and monkeys because their metabolism and . . ."

"For God's sake," said McCullough irritably, "the situation is complicated enough as it is! My idea is this. The dormitories were used by the people who built the Ship, who left when the job was finished. Possibly the compartments will be used for colonists or passengers on a later trip, but not this time. This trip the Ship was, is, on her maiden voyage."

"And since control seems to be largely automatic," Berryman added, "the crew could be very small indeed."

"I want you all to listen to this tape," McCullough said, then added apologetically, "again."

They listened again to the gobbling of Twos in the enclosure, the chiming and moaning and the two alien voices. Like the Twos, they could disregard one of the voices and its accompanying chimes since this was almost certainly some kind of recorded pre-takeoff warning sequence. The moaning could have been caused by machinery, perhaps malfunctioning equipment of some kind, except that no machine should ever make a noise like that. Hollis and Berryman suggested that it might be music of some kind being played in the second voice's quarters. The sound could have been made by a number of wind instruments, but the tonal range and scale were crazy.

So, in all probability, was the alien.

"I'm beginning to think there is only one intelligent e-t left on the Ship," McCullough said as they prepared to leave the compartment, "and that one is in very poor shape physically and mentally. But to help it we need more information about its world and its society, its relations with its fellows or with members of the opposite sex, or sexes if there are more than two, and as much data as we can possibly obtain on its own personal background. Somewhere in the Ship there must be family photographs . . ."

"Psychotherapy is a chancy business," said Berryman quietly, "even with human beings. Trying it on an emotionally disturbed alien seems—seems . . ."

"Foolhardy," said Hollis.

Drew did not say anything. Since the time McCullough had revived him with the Kiss of Life he had never disagreed with the doctor. But occasionally, as now, his face became more than usually expressionless.

To make successful contact with it, McCullough told himself firmly, they would have to see that it was capable of rational behaviour and show that they themselves were friendly toward it. Clearing the Ship of the majority of its Twos should prove their good intentions, but only if the being was sane enough to appreciate and understand what they were doing. And it possessed, or had possessed, a weapon. Why then did it not come out of hiding and help them exterminate the Twos?

They needed more information. The trouble was they had to fight for every single datum and it could be only a matter of time before some perhaps unimportant scrap of information cost someone their life.

But the material they were sending back to Control was valuable. The reports and photographs of alien food labels with pictures and text would send language experts the world over into multilingual paroxysms of joy, not to mention the methods used to make friends with the Three life-form and their subsequent activities together. There was also a steady flow of information on Ship equipment and control systems which would be nonobjectionable so far as Brady was concerned.

They could not, of course, tell him everything. Some of their troubles they had to keep to themselves.

Hollis took to crying in his sleep, during the rare occasions when he was able to get any. Drew collected and trained more Three pets than was really necessary for self-protection. When he moved he was surrounded by a flapping phalanx of Threes and, prior to going to sleep, he stroked and patted them until they had him enclosed in a thick, furry cocoon. Berryman and McCullough watched each other covertly and talked about their physical and psychological problems both as individuals and as a group, the meanings behind the nightmares to which everyone was subject, and their past lives public and private—all with a simulated objectivity which fooled neither of them. Each was waiting for the other one to break and each gained strength because the break did not come.

The times they each woke up struggling and screaming did not count, of course, because they all did that.

Walters, too, was unhappy. Cut off from home

except by voice contact with Prometheus Control, all of whom now sounded more nervous and insincere while talking to him than he felt while talking to them, it was obvious that the pilot was desperately concerned for the safety of his friends—his only friends—on the Ship. During their infrequent radio contacts—it was just not possible these days for McCullough to visit him—the strain in his voice was an almost tangible thing.

The general and Tokyo Rose were beginning to worry him again. They were suggesting that the facts supporting McCullough's theory about the Ship's builders using the dormitory compartments would also support his own, perhaps more logical theory, that the tubular hammocks were meant to contain a couple of Twos, and that it was the Twos who were the crew of the Ship all the time. Walters did not want to bother the doctor with this kind of talk, but sometimes the general made it sound very believable.

Walters was beginning to hate the general actively, and it showed in his voice.

chapter twenty

THEN ONE DAY they were forced to take cover in a room which was more thoroughly furnished, in the esthetic as well as the structural sense, than any they had encountered before. The room contained just two tubular hammocks, its cabinets and fixtures were much less utilitarian than usual, and there were a great many pictures on the walls. And softly, in the background, there was the moaning, whistling sound which they had heard only once before but could never forget.

But in this compartment the structural skeleton did not show and the metal bones and circulatory system were too well concealed by paneling for them to hook up a suit radio antenna to a section of plumbing which would allow contact with Walters. As a result, McCullough could not tell the pilot of the tremendous discovery they had made or bring him into the discussion which followed it.

"Crew quarters, no doubt about it," Hollis said, waving his arms in excitement. "But I don't think this room is only for sleeping in—its furniture is too diversified, there are too many pictures. Crowding a bedroom with pictures is in questionable taste . . ."

"So," said Berryman, "is having twin beds."

"Be serious a minute," said Hollis. "The point I'm trying to make is that there is more than enough space in the Ship for crew members to have different rooms for sleeping, eating, recreation and so on, while this compartment—a surprisingly small room in a very large ship—appears to combine the functions of all three. I may be jumping to conclusions here, but it suggests to me that they prefer small, confined, cozy living quarters. This place looks like—like an illustrated nest or—I give up."

Berryman said, "I am only an amateur psychologist—a gifted amateur, naturally—but I'm inclined to agree with that. The question is, if the crew prefers to live in cozy little rooms inside a great big ship—and with wild Twos roaming the corridors, who could blame them?—why aren't they at home?"

From the door's transparent panel Drew, who was keeping watch, said, "The Twos are beginning to leave. A Three just went by, one of the carpets we haven't made friends with yet, and they took off after it. Can I close the door?"

"Not yet," said McCullough.

He had been too busy with his camera to join in the discussion and his mind had been vainly trying to emulate the instrument by absorbing everything he could see at once. But he was not so wildly excited and curious as to forget caution, or his own fairly well supported theory of the e-t crew member being mentally disturbed and in possession of a projectile-firing weapon. They might be in much more danger from the intelligent alien than from the hungry Twos, and McCullough had ordered the sliding door to be kept partly open in case they should have to leave in a hurry.

McCullough cleared his throat and said, "At the risk of sounding like General Brady, I suggest that the mass of important new data which has been made available should be very carefully considered before we make a move toward communicating with one of the crew."

With the exception of Drew they all returned to the study of the room's fittings. They reminded each other several times that they were examining what were almost certainly personal effects which should be treated with great care. Sometimes they laughed for no apparent reason, or shouted in excitement, or spoke in guilty whispers in case someone or something overheard them.

As well as the medicine cabinet with its Three symbol, there were wall racks to which were clipped surprisingly Earthlike spools of tape or film. Another cabinet held books which were not illustrated, much to the men's disappointment, and yet another contained flexible plastic tubes full of liquid and semiliquid substances which smelled to high heaven.

"Probably booze or beauty cream," said Berryman as he wriggled out of an alien bed. He had been investigating the interiors of both hammocks. When his legs were clear he added, "They're almost comfortable if it wasn't for the dampness and smell. When you push against the inside the padding secretes something which smells like—like . . . It's a damp smell, not altogether unpleasant."

McCullough investigated with eye and nose, finding that he had to push away several of the Threes to do so. But the animals were wriggling and flapping around only one of the hammocks. He was reminded suddenly of dogs excited by the scent of their master or by the clothing or personal possessions of their master. One of these beds had been occupied recently, he felt sure, or the Threes would not be so excited. He turned back to look again at the pictures.

Most of them showed pallid, leafless vegetation set against a dark, mottled background or one that resembled rough-grained wood. While there was a definite feeling of depth to the pictures, there was no middle distance or horizon, and McCullough assumed that they were some kind of still-life studies. But there were two pictures which had everything— size, perspective and almost photographic detail. One of them showed the plant or thing or whatever it was that they had at first mistaken for a multicolored pile of spaghetti, with trees in the foreground and clouds behind to give a true indication of its tremendous size. Another showed trees with strange leaves on them, thick, wiry undergrowth harboring a running Two and a dazzlingly bright sky. A great many questions regarding the Two life-form were answered by that picture.

The e-t stag at bay, he thought drily.

He could now tell General Brady that the Twos were, in fact, animals and not intelligent beings. While this knowledge would be a load off everyone's mind, it still meant that McCullough was faced with the problem of making contact with the intelligent extraterrestrial on the Ship, and all at once he was most horribly afraid and unsure of himself. He did not want the responsibility and he could not make the decision which was being forced on him—at least, not right now.

In a couple of hours, perhaps, or days . . .

Right now he wanted to slap an indefinite Hold on everything. He wanted time to look at all the evidence old and new, and discuss it quietly and in the greatest possible detail. This time he could not afford to push the wrong psychological button, for he was now firmly convinced that there was only one intelligent extraterrestrial left in the Ship and that physically and emotionally it was not in good shape.

It took a tremendous effort for him to make his voice sound firm and steady when he spoke.

"Everybody out," he said. "We must report this to Brady and decide on our next move. This time we can't afford to make a mistake. Collect your Threes and let's go. Quickly!"

But the Threes did not want to leave. It took more than ten minutes' coaxing and petting to make them leave the vicinity of that one cylindrical hammock. Meanwhile Drew reported Twos beginning to gather a little way along the corridor and asked permission to close the door, and Berryman, his Threes covering his body like a form-fitting fur coat, continued to look around.

Suddenly he called, "Over here!"

The pilot had opened what he thought was the door of a recessed cupboard—there were a number of them in the room—and found himself looking along a short stretch of corridor. There was another door containing a large transparent panel at the other end, and beyond that another room which was in darkness except for the myriads of indicator lights burning like regimented stars on the facing wall. As they watched, a black shadow began to occlude some of the stars.

"Outside!" shouted McCullough again. "Quickly,

and make sure the door is closed properly behind us!"

"But there's dozens of them out here," said Drew angrily. "Something is biting them. I've never heard Twos make a noise like this before."

"Get out of here!"

When the entrance to the alien crew's compartment was safely closed behind him, McCullough tried to explain why he had insisted on them leaving a relatively safe position for their present highly dangerous one, but they were all too angry to talk and there were so many Twos in the corridor that they couldn't risk taking their eyes off them even to look at him. Probably they were hating him for being stupid or a coward, or both. But McCullough, while scared stiff of meeting the alien face to face, had been even more afraid of another possibility. He had suddenly thought of the animal enclosure with its half-eaten body of the other crew member, and he had had a picture of what the Twos would do if they broke into that last compartment.

He wondered if the alien had considered his reaction cowardly, always supposing that the being was capable of reasoning at all. But even if grief over the loss of what was very probably its mate, and loneliness and fear inside this vast, Two-infested Ship—and possibly physical injuries as well—had driven it insane or close to insanity, a cowardly reaction might actually be reassuring to it. There was nobody who helped a coward like an even greater coward. But he could not cure the alien, or communicate with it, by running away all the time.

On Earth, psychiatric treatment of seriously disturbed patients—insane was not considered a nice word—had had only limited success, so what chance had a doctor, who was not even a psychologist, of curing a patient whose archetypal images were out of this world, whose phallic symbols were unrecognizable, and whose culture contained in all probability a welter of psychological theories even more complex and mutually contradictory than those current on Earth? There might be some relatively simple form of therapy possible, of course. The e-t equivalent of the snake pit where the patient cured itself with just a little, unskilled help and a lot of sympathy.

But that was asking for too much. Right now McCullough needed specialist advice and assistance, from Earth.

"Back to the hull lock chamber," he said. "We have to contact Walters, and Brady. Hurry it up!"

The Twos attacked while he was speaking, filling the corridor with colliding, cartwheeling bodies and slashing, horn-tipped tentacles. In the confusion Drew and Hollis got three of them and Berryman one before they were able to pull clear of the mêlée. McCullough seriously wounded a couple of them and lost contact with his Three after the furry creature had started to strangle another Two which had been trying to swarm onto his back. But suddenly it was with him again, flapping along behind him as they retreated along the corridor. He reached back, caught it and pulled it onto his shoulders like a great, furry cape.

Suddenly they were trapped. Another group of Twos came boiling out of an intersection ahead of them, bouncing off the wall netting and each other like outsize, tentacled molecules illustrating the Brownian movement of gases. Obviously the humans had not reduced the number of Twos as efficiently as they had hoped.

Berryman shouted, "In here!"

He was holding open the sliding door into a large dormitory compartment and they went through it backward, spears jabbing at full extension, fighting off Twos. Seconds after they had slid it shut, the door bulged alarmingly as several Twos charged it together, but it did not come off its runners. Drew and Berryman were able to get their spears through the warped outsides of the door and stab attacking Twos with comparative safety and they killed four of the animals without, however, seriously discouraging the attack. Hollis and McCullough, meanwhile, made a quick check of the compartment. Their most important discoveries were another exit and, floating in one of the corners, a thick, illustrated magazine.

The color reproduction and values were strange and the printed characters even stranger, not to mention the raised, embossed pattern on the bottom outside corner of each page which allowed them to be turned by alien digits terminating in osseus material, but somehow it still managed to look like a copy of an illustrated magazine that might have been picked up anywhere on Earth. McCullough longed for time to examine it and discuss it at length with the others. He wanted to photograph it page by page and have Walters transmit the pictures to Earth and have everyone there discuss it and offer specialist advice.

But behind him the Twos were battering their way through the warped sliding door. McCullough folded the magazine carefully and wedged it between his air tanks and his back, then led the way out of the other exit and along the corridor.

They continued to duck in and out of compartments, some of which were large, interconnected dormitories with several exits, and for several minutes they completely lost the Twos. By then they were completely lost themselves.

"Berryman," said McCullough, steadying himself against a hammock as he tried to catch his mental and physical breath. "Check the plumbing with a view to contacting Walters. Hollis, help him. While you're doing so, try to think of a quick way of repairing the sabotaged generator. Drew, stay by the door. To save time I'll begin taping a report for the general while you two try to contact P-One."

But the Twos battered down the door a few minutes later and they were forced to move again.

Drew swore horribly and said that he did not know what had got into them. Normally ferocious and blindly antagonistic, they were now literally killing themselves, cracking open their bony carapaces against the metal doors and running into each others' horns in their attempts to get at the humans. It was as if some dreadful hysteria had them in its grip and the grip was tightening by the minute.

Some very special kind of killing instinct was being aroused, McCullough told himself as the men were forced to flee once again. It had to be a very deep-rooted instinct because these Twos were almost certainly second or third generation.

The report was finally completed during a lull while the Twos, who were still in the grip of the conditioning which made them visit the food dispensers at mealtimes, were absent. Berryman identified a section of plumbing belonging to the hydraulic system actuating the hull cargo locks and said that it should make a very good link with their ship. The pilot quickly connected his suit radio antenna, said that someone was already talking at the other end, and turned up the volume.

Tinny, distorted and furiously angry, Brady's voice rattled out at them.

"... *What you said was bad enough. Thoughtless, irresponsible, downright criminal considering the political situation here—and I'm disregarding the tone, which was insubordinate to the point of mutiny! But those pictures, that cold-blooded slaughter of what are almost certainly intelligent beings—you've been secretive, McCullough is afraid even to talk to me, and no wonder! Killing Twos has been reduced to a fine art, and judging by those pictures...*"

"Walters—" began McCullough.

"... *enjoying practicing that art! You act like barbarians instead of so-called reasoning beings! And you can't even claim the excuse of honest insanity, because your actions are too cold-blooded and carefully thought out. Moral cowardice, which is not an excuse, and megalomania is what ails you all—you made a mistake, McCullough made a mistake with the Twos at the onset and will slaughter every last one of them rather than admit it! I want to talk to you, Doctor. I know you're afraid to listen but...*"

"Turn him down, Walters, I want to talk to you ..."

"... *All things being equal the simple rather than the complicated explanation is usually the true one! Try THIS theory, Doctor. It was evolved by people here who know their stuff, and it also fits the facts. The Ship dormitory accommodation was meant for its large complement of Twos—it may have been a colonization project, a troop transport, or it may simply have needed a very large crew. A couple of Twos could squeeze into those hammocks, you know—have you considered that? Then something happened during the early part of the trip, after the*

*course had already been set for this solar system.
Whatever catastrophe occurred, it was almost certainly nonphysical. The end result was a process of
cultural devolution which brought the crew close to
the level of animals. They broke into, not out of, the
animal cages in search of food and eventually sank
to practicing cannibalism. But they did not forget all
their early training—or their ancestors' early training—because they reacted violently toward anyone
who appeared to threaten their Ship.*

*I can even make a prediction based on this theory,
McCullough. It is this. The closer you approach the
Ship's control center—which the Twos must regard
as some sort of mystic shrine or taboo area by now,
since they know it is vital to the Ship without understanding why—their antagonism toward you will increase . . ."*

Berryman, Hollis and Drew were staring at him,
faces chalk-white and reflecting the same horrible
fear and guilt and confusion that was gripping
McCullough. He couldn't be so *wrong,* he told himself desperately. He didn't have to listen to this . . .

*". . . Beyond appeals to reason. The world is judging us, your country and everyone in it, by your
actions. But you don't care about that, do you?
Well, we don't care about you! Believe me, if we
directed the two remaining supply rockets off course
we would not be too strongly criticized for doing so.
We're ashamed of you, McCullough, and the rest of
your murdering pack—you're little more than mad
dogs! You sicken and disgust us . . ."*

Brady's voice began to fade as Walters on P-One
reduced the volume. But not soon enough.

*". . . Nobody here wants you, d'you understand
that? We don't want to see you back!"*

chapter twenty-one

MENTAL ANGUISH COULD take many forms, McCullough thought sickly, ranging from simple worry over a possible future unpleasantness to the deep grief at the loss of a dear one. But those were clean, uncomplicated emotions whatever their degree of intensity—*this* was the twisting, almost physical pain of betrayal by a trusted friend who turns suddenly into an enemy and raised to the nth power. For it was not only their personal friends at Prometheus who had betrayed and rejected them, it was their whole lousy race!

From the shocked, angry faces all around him McCullough knew that only two reactions were possible. Anger and counterattack or extreme, soul-destroying guilt and despair. But they had come through too much together on the Ship, they had overcome too many purely physical dangers for them to die of a collective broken heart. He told himself that this was so, but he was not sure that he could believe himself. He could not be sure of anything any more.

A metallic crash from the door told of the Twos, even angrier probably because the food dispensers were no longer giving food, beginning to return from lunch. He wondered suddenly if intelligent beings could sink so low as to eat animal food, and thought they might if something had happened to the crew water and food supply. But Brady's theory was too simple, surely. There were facts that it did not explain, and one fact in particular was deafeningly obvious.

"I'm not a psychologist," said McCullough quietly, trying to control his relief and excitement, "but it seems to me that the last thing an intelligent person would forget is how to open and close a door." He turned to the radio and went on quickly, "So you showed him pictures of us dumping Twos into space, but I can guess at some of the things he said to make you do it, so don't worry. Just link me with the transmitter, Walters, there is something I want to say to him . . ."

He had begun by speaking quietly to the pilot, and his voice was still soft. But the anger that crept into it when he spoke to the general made it unrecognizable even to himself.

"We feel sorry for you, General Brady," he said, "we feel sorry for *all* you people. It would be a lie to say that we don't feel angry and disgusted with you as well, but we do feel sorry. The harsh facts of contact with an extraterrestrial culture are being brought home to you, to *all* of you. *And you are all frightened.* The implications are only now beginning to dawn on you and you feel guilty and ashamed because things may not have been handled right. It is a very uncomfortable time for all of you, and your feelings and qualms of conscience do you credit. But you, General, and all of you, are so uncomfortable that you want to avoid both the responsibility and the guilt by passing it onto us. Then, presumably, you will bury and forget the whole thing by disowning us!"

"There is nothing original about this course," McCullough went on. "It is a clear case of your eyes and your hands scandalizing you, and you then quote the highest possible Authority regarding your subsequent action in the matter. If your right eye scandalize thee, pluck it out. If your right hand scandalize thee, cut it off and cast it from thee, and so on. But if you were thinking straight, you would realize that this is not a true analogy. We are not just your hands and eyes, we are a cross-section of all the people of Earth. *That* is what's really bothering you, and you know it! What we feel toward the aliens is what you would feel in the same circumstances, our thoughts would be your thoughts, our actions and reactions yours as well. You know this is true but you don't want to face up to it. Instead you are making us the scapegoat.

"We are doing the best we can with the situation here," he continued more quietly. "We are better qualified to understand it, since we are on the spot, and we are convinced that we are doing the right thing. A tape containing much valuable new information has been prepared. This will be placed in a Two-proof storage cabinet and played back to you while we head for the hull to repair the damaged generator. While this is being done, Twos permitting, we shall make contact with the surviving intelligent members, or more likely member, of the Ship's crew.

"In the meantime, General, lay off Walters! What you're doing to him is criminal and stupid. He is not responsible for our actions inside the Ship. He is all alone, cut off from radio contact with us for days on end, not knowing whether we are alive or dead and now believing that *you* don't care what happens to him. If you can't appreciate his position, ask your space medics—he must be clinging to sanity by his fingernails!

"You might also consider *our* position. There are only two functioning spacesuits left to us, we're constantly under attack or being forced to hide from Twos and some of us haven't slept for three days. Now you have turned against us and are threatening to turn the supply vehicles off course. At best your remarks, if indeed you meant them, are totally unstatesmanlike; at worst, criminally irresponsible. We're a long way from home and you've literally got us outnumbered billions to one. If those replacement suits don't arrive we can never leave this Ship . . ."

McCullough broke off. He was beginning to whine and the realization made him angry. He could see the weary despair in the expressions of the others as they watched him, and hear the Twos stepping up their attack on the door. But this was not the reason why he raised his voice.

"If you maroon us here, either by accident or design, there is something you should bear in mind. We have lived on e-t food and recycled water since the last supply vehicle went wide. The food is palatable if one is hungry enough and the taste of the water is due only to our thinking too much about its original source. So we can stay here if necessary. We can go back with the Ship to its home planet and—and see things that nobody in all of human history has seen before.

"So you can't reject us, General," he ended furiously. "Or cast us off or do anything at all to us, because we damn well *quit*!"

A few minutes later they left by the other exit, moving in what they hoped was the direction of the hull and the generator blister. From the suit radios of Berryman and Hollis, McCullough's voice came as a tinny, stereophonic duet as they monitored the tape transmission. Should it cease, that would mean that the storage cabinet containing the linked radio and recorder was not as Two-proof as they had hoped.

"*. . . Already treated design and structural philosophy in detail,*" the voice was saying, "*and our deductions regarding the home planet's gravity, atmospheric conditions and environment have been supported by pictures on living quarters walls and in illustrated literature. Regarding these living quarters, however . . .*"

"Which way?" said Berryman. "I don't know whether we're headed forward, outboard or aft . . ."

McCullough could hear the Twos breaking their way out of the compartment they had just vacated—the things were like extraterrestrial bloodhounds! He said, "Right, I think . . ."

"*. . . Construction personnel lived on board and vacated their quarters, which are rather stark, when the project was complete. The large number of empty storage compartments, living quarters and, most of all, the fact that entry hatches and lighting circuits tend to be on local rather than centralized control,*"

*and that there are no indications of permanent com-
munication lines between compartments, makes us
sure that they were used only by the construction
gang.*

*"The strongest probability is that the large size of
the Ship was dictated by the operating requirements
of its hyperdrive generators and that in this, its first
flight, it has been operating as an interstellar probe
containing automatic guidance and sensory equipment and a number of animals being tested for
survival in space conditions together with a small
crew who were little more than intelligent specimens
undergoing the same testing. Indications are that the
'crew' have virtually no control over the operation of
the Ship, and that initially they numbered only
two. . ."*

They were in a long corridor which seemed to be
going in the wrong direction. Every Two in the Ship
seemed to be after them, but just out of sight.

*". . . We assumed the Two life-form to be unintel-
ligent because they showed no indication of possess-
ing an organized language, no manual dexterity in
opening and closing doors or operating light switches
and no inclination to communicate. Here we must
mention our belief that an intelligent species making
contact for the first time would make allowances for
a certain amount of, to them, unconventional behavior and would not react with such continual and
violent hostility. In the light of this assumption we
will consider the situation in the animal enclosure
. . ."*

"If we were moving outboard there should be
more intersections," said Hollis. "One at every deck
level, in fact."

The Twos were in sight behind them again,

boiling along the corridor like tumbleweeds in a hurricane, bouncing from wall net to wall net as their tentacles hurled them on. Unlike the humans, they did not worry about hurting themselves or protecting the two remaining usable spacesuits, so they were gaining steadily.

"... obvious that the Twos broke out and virtually exterminated all other animal life-forms with the exception of the Threes which, although nonhostile where we and the intelligent e-t life-form are concerned, can defend themselves against the Twos. The Twos bred unrestrained, living off the automatic food dispensers and any other experimental animal which had escaped the initial slaughter, their numbers controlled by their habit of fighting and eating each other.

"One of the half-eaten carcasses in the animal enclosure belonged to a large, caterpillar-like life-form which was quite obviously unsuited to the cage in which it was found. Around it were the bodies of Twos which, in addition to being cannibalized, showed numerous punctured wounds in musculature and bone structure of the kind made by a solid projectile-firing weapon.

"It is now obvious that this caterpillar life-form, which later data proves to be intelligent, was killed trying to contain the original breakout. The weapon may have been used by this being against the Twos and later retrieved by the second intelligent e-t from its body, or the second e-t used it in an attempt to rescue or avenge the first one . . ."

"No good," said Hollis breathlessly as he ducked out of yet another useless compartment. "Only one door."

The room might have given them indefinite protection if they could have defended the door against Twos, but there were no wall nets inside storage and dormitory compartments and no means of bracing themselves against attack. If the Twos succeeded in battering their way in, the result would be a shambles of twisting, spinning bodies and stabbing, slashing spears and tentacles and most of the casualties would be on the human side.

If they had to fight Twos it was better done in a corridor.

". . . Before listing the data and reasoning which leads us to believe that there were only two intelligent e-t's crewing the Ship, and that one of them still survives in a physically and mentally damaged condition, we must deal with what is known and deduced about their home planet's environment and culture . . ."

At McCullough's signal they checked themselves against the wall net, faced inward and laced their feet and legs through the strands so as not to be torn free during the attack. The butts of their spears were jammed against the net's supporting brackets or any other convenient projection and they waited, McCullough thought, for all the world like a bunch of medieval foot soldiers about to soak up a cavalry charge.

"Since we left the crew's quarters—" began Hollis, then finished with a rush, "I think we picked up some kind of scent in there. It's driving them mad— I recognize Twos we wounded a couple of weeks ago, and every blasted Two in the Ship must be after us. This is a good chance for us to wipe them out completely. . ."

"Have you *counted* them?" said Berryman bitterly.

"Sixteen," said Drew.

"... whose gravity, pressure and atmospheric composition is similar to Earth's—which is probably the chief reason for the Ship's presence here. Observation of pictures of planetary flora and fauna suggest a world subject to frequent or perhaps constant high winds ..."

The leading Twos were only yards and split seconds away.

chapter twenty-two

THEY COULD NOT be sure where exactly the Threes and Ones fitted into the picture, but the position of the intelligent caterpillars and the Twos was now plain. The scarcity of Ones indicated that most of their number had succumbed to the carnivorous instincts of the Twos.

The tentacled animal with the single, underslung horn was a carnivore, of course, and the natural enemy of the intelligent e-t's. They had adapted well to weightless conditions, but on the home planet their normal method of locomotion was to use the large, curved horn as a sort of skid while propelling themselves with their tentacles. The skid also served as a weapon when jumping onto their prey or, when plunged into soft ground during periods of high wind, as an anchor which allowed the Two to seize smaller animals with its tentacles as they blew helplessly past.

The plant life was uniformly alien.

Smaller plants consisted of a long, flexible stem

which, because of the wind, lay on or close to the ground. The stem carried a number of large, thick leaves with thorns or rootlets on their undersides and seemed to combine the process of photosynthesis with the digestion of ground-burrowing insects. At the other end of the scale were the giant trees towering hundreds of feet into the air, with trunks fifty feet in diameter and massive, stubby branches in proportion.

Because of their tremendous thickness the trunks and branches bent only slightly in the wind. Their leaves were enormous aerofoils controlled either by the vegetable nervous system of the tree or by some automatic stabilizer system in the leaf itself, so that they streamed out to leeward while maintaining a formation which kept every leaf in sunshine.

The leaves were the only opaque parts of the trees. Trunk and branches were translucent except for dark areas occurring at irregular intervals which could have been parasitic growths or caused by small animals being dashed against the trunk by the wind. Other dark patches were various forms of animal life existing inside the trees.

Another growth or structure which had puzzled them until pictures became available which gave a true indication of its size was the heap of varicolored, translucent spaghetti. This mass appeared flexible and open enough for the wind to blow through it without putting too much strain on the individual tubes, which divided and subdivided at intervals and contained hundreds of bulbous swellings along their length before rejoining into a single stem again or linking up with another stem. From the top of this squirming and strangely beautiful mass hundreds of metallic blooms on ridiculously thin stems trailed in the wind. Eventually they realized that they were seeing an alien city, a great, artificial tree with trailing windmill blooms supplying power to a structure which must extend a considerable depth below the surface.

The wind was such an integral part of the aliens' lives that on the Ship the sounds it made were played like background music ...

". . . Originally the intelligent e-t's must have developed from a species of burrowing tree dweller. Physically they resemble outsize, leathery caterpillars whose heads are very well supplied with teeth which now show signs of advanced atrophication, and they have four mandibles terminating in flexible digits which appear both strong and highly sensitive . . ."

The first one came at them along the center of the corridor, shell first like a tentacled cannonball. Their spears were useless against that bony carapace so they flattened themselves against the net and let it sail past. The next one came spinning at them edge on and tentacles flailing, close to the wall occupied by Drew. He guided his spear into the soft area below the edge of the shell and between the tentacles and the momentum of the Two's dive did the rest. He pitchforked the dying animal down the corridor, and then they were all very busy.

". . . this deeply rooted racial agoraphobia—they are burrowers, after all, even if they do burrow through nearly transparent trees. The murals, illustrations and especially the close-fitting hammocks support this.

"It could be argued that the process of overcoming this agoraphobia and achieving the level of technology evident here was a slow one, which means that

*they could be much farther advanced in the sociolog-
ical sciences than we are, and a peaceful first contact
would be possible if it wasn't for the suspected mental damage . . ."*

They came at them two and three at a time,
seeming to fill the corridor from wall to wall with
flailing tentacles and long, twitching, obscene horns.
McCullough got his spear to a vital spot but in the
act of pushing the furiously dying thing away he felt
a tentacle crash excruciatingly against his legs. When
he could see again, there was a Two crawling up his
legs and he had too long a hold on his weapon for it
to bear. He twisted frantically to the side, pulled one
leg out of the net and drew it up until the knee
touched his chin, then stamped down hard on the
base of the Two's horn. Reaction from the blow
dislodged his other foot from the net, but the kick
must have inflicted severe internal damage because
the Two went into violent convulsions and died.

"Dirty fighting, sir," said Drew, who had just
finished off another by more conventional methods.
"I must remember that trick . . ."

Both his legs were sticking out into the corridor
and before McCullough could swing them back, another Two grabbed his foot. This time the spear
would bear all right, but he jabbed himself in the leg
before he was able to kill it. Strangely the only pain
he felt was one of loss—there was only one functioning spacesuit left now. But there was no time to
think about that for long. The corridor was a solid
mass of struggling alien and human bodies, a nightmare of tentacles, legs, arms, furry carpets, stabbing
horns and spears. And over the high-pitched gobblings and furious voices of the combatants there

was the quiet voice of McCullough expounding his theories regarding alien psychology . . .

". . . *So far as we can tell, the Two life-form is the enemy of everything which lives and moves, but particularly of the intelligent e-t's who made up the crew of the Ship. It is small wonder, then, that the single remaining alien refuses to come out of its quarters, and that a high level of fear must be added to the loneliness and lack of support from its fellows which it is suffering—feelings which we ourselves are in a very good position to appreciate. If we also assume them to belong to a bisexual race—and there is no evidence against this—then the crew were probably mated . . .*"

McCullough fended off a violently dying alien with a Three on its back and saw that Drew was in serious trouble. He had lost his spear and a Two had its tentacles wrapped around his hips and waist. He was trying frantically to push it off him, both hands flat against its underbelly and arms stiffened. This was how Morrison had died, McCullough thought sickly as he swung up his spear and took careful aim so as not to stab Drew.

But before he could do anything, a second Two landed on Drew's back and drove its horn in deep. Drew's arms went limp and he was caught, sandwiched and impaled between the two of them. For an instant he looked appealingly at McCullough, his face yellow-white with shock, and tried to say something. But only blood came out and McCullough killed both Twos without worrying about jabbing Drew.

Then suddenly the corridor was clear. The Twos

had dived and spun and blundered their way past and the half dozen or so that had survived were clinging to the netting a short distance along the corridor, preparing to attack again.

"... If the crew member has lost its mate, especially if the survivor is the weaker or less technically qualified of the two, this would further aggravate its emotionally disturbed condition as well as explain the lack of interference during our exploration.

"There is also a strong possibility that the survivor is physically as well as mentally damaged, but it is, of course, the mental aspect which concerns us at the present time ..."

"Here they come," said Berryman in a voice which was too weary to show emotion. McCullough dragged his eyes away from the gruesome three-body problem which was Drew, and tried desperately to pretend that none of this was happening, that soon he would wake up somewhere, anywhere, else.

But he did not wake up and the Twos rushed down on him, figments of a nightmare which was not even of Earth. Their tentacles spread and coiled like the legs of great, fat spiders and that horrible, obscene horn jabbed and quivered and gave every attack the added horror of indecent assault.

"... Psychology is far from being an exact science, and it is difficult enough to cure the aberrations of a human being ..."

Twice his spear made a wet, thudding sound and another pair of Twos spun out of sight. He began to think that they might, after all, succeed in exterminating the animals. It was obvious that they were all here, attracted by the scent the humans had picked up in the crew quarters. With the Twos out of the way they could investigate the Ship at leisure, building up a picture of the culture of its home planet and getting to know and understand the alien crew member before actual contact was attempted. But then everything went suddenly wrong.

Berryman speared a Two just as another came spinning close to the net on McCullough's side. The doctor lunged, missed and had to fend it off with his feet. Both animals crashed together just as a third arrived on the scene, and within seconds the remainder of the Twos were adding to the pile-up. McCullough lost his spear—he couldn't bring it to bear anyway—and somebody screamed and then went on cursing. McCullough wanted to laugh because that meant the wound had not been immediately fatal.

He threw his arms around a passing Two, hugging its bony shell close to his chest so that its horn and threshing tentacles formed a defensive shield. He shouted, "Get out of here! Crawl along the wall net, get *clear*!"

They kicked and wrestled their way free of the jam, Berryman first, then Hollis and McCullough trailed by their madly flapping Threes. Already the First Twos were beginning to give chase.

"We have to find shelter," Berryman gasped as they sailed along the corridor. "A good, strong door . . ."

Hollis was looking back over his shoulder. He said, "Only—only five of them left . . ."

"In here!"

Berryman had stopped and was clinging to the net beside a door, one arm out to check Hollis. They pulled the door aside and within seconds the pilot's head, shoulders and spear showed around the edge as he prepared to defend it until the others arrived.

Behind them the Twos went suddenly berserk.

"No!" McCullough shouted urgently. *"Berryman, get out of there!"*

But it was too late. A Two hurled itself past both Hollis and himself without bothering even to strike at them. It impaled itself on Berryman's spear, driving the haft backward between the wall and the sliding panel. Berryman yelled that he couldn't free his spear and the door was jammed open.

Hollis had caught the netting beside the door and was about to go through when McCullough arrived behind him. The doctor gripped the net firmly, planted both feet in the small of the physicist's back and pushed hard. Berryman looked at McCullough as if he had just committed murder.

"Contact Walters!" McCullough yelled as Hollis went spinning down the corridor. "Clear the short in the generator! And don't worry about the Twos— they aren't interested in *you* now!"

They would not follow Hollis because Berryman had just opened another way into the crew quarters.

It was a different entrance, opening into a compartment they had not seen before. One wall was covered with the bright, translucent murals McCullough had come to know so well and the rest of the small room was devoted to storage cabinets. There was a sound of wind blowing through alien trees. It was unoccupied.

McCullough pointed to the room's inner door and said, very seriously, "They mustn't kill the last survivor. We've done enough harm to the Ship as it is. We've got to kill every last one of them here and now . . ."

"... And in conclusion we must state that the surviving e-t, for physical or mental reasons or both, is almost certainly helpless ..."

It was a large doorway and the spear jammed across it did not form an effective barrier. The first attacker blundered onto Berryman's spear, the second batted it aside with one tentacle and reached for him with the other three. With no net to steady him, suspended weightless and helpless in the middle of the room, Berryman was being pulled onto its horn when a Three got between them and was caught instead. It fluttered like a furry flag and died while Berryman struggled free. The rest of the Twos were swarming in.

McCullough took a blow on the shoulder which nearly paralyzed his arm, and suddenly there was a Two with its tentacles around his head and shoulder and its horn only inches away from his face. He let go his spear and grabbed for the horn with both hands. It was dry and hot and felt like rough wood. The whole twitching mass of its underbelly was oily with alien sweat or saliva and the stink made him want to vomit. The room rotated slowly around them as their struggles made them spin.

Berryman swam into sight beside a dying Two. He was terribly wounded and large, red bubbles were forming and breaking away from his abdomen and chest. A Three was trying to spread itself over him so as to stanch the flow of blood, and wriggling because Berryman, an expression on his face that was almost sublime, kept running his fingers through the fur on its back. The pilot swung into sight three or four times before McCullough saw that he had died. And still the doctor gripped the Two's horn and tried desperately to push it away.

But it clung and tightened its hold and hung above his head like a vile, alien umbrella. His legs were encircled and another Two swarmed awkwardly along his body. He tried to kick it away but it was too high up. Then he saw that there was a Three on its back, the flat, furry body oozing between the Two's tentacles, blinding and smothering it in tight, clinging fur until it drifted away dead.

But the Threes were fluttering and flapping all over the compartment, unwilling for some reason to come to his aid. His spear was drifting a few feet away, but he dared not let go of the horn for even a second and expect to live. The Two kept changing its grip and each time the horn came a little closer. His arms were very tired . . .

". . . In general terms its psychological troubles stem from loneliness, grief, and fear caused by its being surrounded by enemies. It must feel that there is nobody who cares whether it lives or dies.

"We know so little about this being that curative therapy is beyond us. But if its basic needs are enough like ours, and if its mental condition has not already reached the point of no return we might, by our actions alone, show it that . . ."

McCullough tried to count slowly to ten. He thought that if he could just hold off that horrible yellow horn for ten seconds he would be able to do it for another ten seconds. But the muscles in his back were cracking and his arms felt as if they were on fire. He closed his eyes tight because he was horribly afraid of seeing as well as feeling himself being killed.

". . . And eventually make it realize that it isn't alone and that someone, us, is trying to help it . . ."

The noise in that confined space was incredible. McCullough jerked open his eyes to see chunks of tentacles and shell being torn off his Two. Then he saw why the Threes were so excited, the weapon with its odd double stock and very ordinary magazine and barrel, and the being who was holding it.

He saw, too, the four manipulators encircling the alien's head, three of which were so badly damaged that it was a miracle it was able to hold the weapon at all, and the awful, Two-inflicted scars running the length of its body. He looked last at its eyes and for a long time neither of them did anything. Then the alien pushed its machine gun away and McCullough, now that his taped report had come to an end, began calling Hollis and Walters on his suit radio.

chapter twenty-three

～～～～～～～

BOTH SUPPLY ROCKETS with their water, food and spare spacesuits went off course.

When he told him about it, Walter's voice was strained. McCullough could imagine the pilot's feelings—the fear of how the doctor might react, his pleas for help which the pilot could not possibly give him, and Walter's own, personal fear of the long voyage home with Hollis in a vehicle which had already passed the time limit for operational safety. When the pilot went on speaking, his cheerfulness was obviously forced.

He said, "Brady feels terrible about this. He says you did the right thing despite his and everyone else's opposition. He's sorry for the things he said to you and he says he deserved everything you said to him. He—well, he's beginning to sound like Churchill —the debt owed you by the whole of humanity, the immeasurable social and scientific advances this First Contact will bring about, and so on. He wishes there was only some way to bring all of us back . . ."

The pilot broke off, then said awkwardly, "You said earlier how terrific a thing it would be to travel to another solar system . . ."

McCullough and Hollis looked at each other and the alien watched both of them. They were in the antechamber of the generator blister where the physicist had just completed repairs, and the e-t had followed them there as it followed them everywhere. Sometimes the being made noises at them or waved its mandible or they exchanged sketches. But mostly it just hung there and watched everything they did.

It was possible that the being was security conscious or anxious lest they commit further acts of sabotage, but McCullough did not think so. To his way of thinking, the e-t was simply glad of the company, any company.

To Walters he said, "It seemed like a fine idea at the time, but I wasn't thinking straight just then. No doubt someone will bust a gut to get going, and it'll happen soon if, as I'm convinced, we can duplicate the Ship's drive. But I prefer to go home."

"But sir . . ."

"Hollis' suit is still in one piece, and I have an idea. Last week it would not have been a good idea . . ."

. . . Because last week Berryman and Drew were alive and both P-ships would have been needed to get them home . . .

By the time he had finished explaining, Walters was much happier. The pilot said briskly, "Two days should be enough for the job, but I'll contact Brady at once asking for a course based on a four-day countdown—that will give us time to check our ship. And —and I'll tell them we want return tickets for three!"

He had to explain his idea to the alien then, but that was not too difficult because the old adage

about a good picture being worth two thousand
words held true even among extraterrestrials. But the
result was that the alien stuck even closer to him
from then on, especially when Hollis was working on
P-One. And it kept forcing things on him, things like
odd pieces of equipment, the lovely, glowing murals
and carvings, books and film spools as well as food
and water. McCullough explained graphically about
fuel reserves and weight allowances and knew that
the alien understood, but it still continued to give
him things.

Then early in the second day Hollis completed his
work on P-One. On the Ship a large cargo hatch
swung open and Walters, moving very slowly and
carefully, edged toward it. The two P-ships were
docked nose to nose and Hollis had stripped P-One
of all its projecting antennae, collectors and sensory
equipment and had completely removed the return
fuel tanks and motors so that the bare command
module would fit, just nicely, int the large cargo lock.

Walters slid the stripped-down P-One into the cargo lock, detached it from P-Two and withdrew. The
outer seal was closed and pressure restored. Hollis,
McCullough and the alien began transferring quan-
tites of food, water, artifacts, photographs and
sketches which they had placed in the corridor into
the module section. Then they wedged it firmly into
the lock chamber—a present from Earth for a culture an unguessable number of light-years away—
and suddenly it was time to go.

It had been relatively easy to exchange simple
concepts via sketch pad, but there was no way at all
for him to tell what it was thinking during those last
few minutes in the airlock. It was just a great, fat
caterpillar, an LSD nightmare with too many eyes

and mouths in all the wrong places, for him to be able to read such a subtle thing as a facial expression—and the problem cut both ways. All he could do was look at it for a few minutes while it looked at him, then follow Hollis into P-One.

The cargo hatch swung open, air whistled into space and Walters came edging back with P-Two. He docked, they transferred themselves and their stores and artifacts into P-Two and drifted away again. The cargo hatch closed, Walters used steering thrust briefly and the great Ship fell slowly away from them.

For a long time McCullough did not speak. He was thinking about the alien he had just left and its Ship and the beings who had sent her out, and wondering what they would think of his people—the people who had left three of their dead aboard, killed while trying to clear the Ship of a particularly nasty form of vermin. And in one of the cargo locks there was a human artifact, a tiny, ridiculous, fragile shell which had carried three human beings more than fifty million miles out to their Ship. He did not know what they would think about his people, but that P-ship should tell them a lot.

Walters had completed a last altitude check and was listening to Control during the last few seconds of the countdown when the generator blisters on the Ship glowed suddenly. In an instant it had shrunk from sight.

Hollis gave a great sigh of relief. "I was worried in case I'd botched the repair job," he said. Then he looked closely at McCullough and added, "Don't worry, Doctor, our friend will be all right. It's going home."

Walters was moving his lips silently. Suddenly he pressed the thrust button and said, "So are we . . ."

ROBERT A. HEINLEIN